# SAVING

# MERCY

∞

NICOLE TILLMAN

*Dedicated to Tobias and Chandler.*

# Chapter One

## Ryan

My eyelids sprang open with vigor for the first time in almost a month. That was my first clue that something was wrong. Something besides the fact that I was waking up on the cold linoleum floor of the kitchen instead of my comfortable full-sized bed.

Pushing myself off the floor, I threaded my fingers together before lifting my arms above my head and glancing around the apartment. Nothing was out of place. The weather was just the same as it had been the day before. And as always, I was alone. It was the same drab scene as always, but something felt *different*. Everything seemed brighter, more focused, and eerily quiet.

And that's when it hit me...

I wasn't in pain.

The sunlight filtering in through my makeshift curtains didn't slice through my skull as it had the day before. The sound of the garbage truck outside didn't rattle my cerebral tissue to the point of nausea. And blissfully, I didn't feel the need to reach for the bottle of painkillers on my nightstand.

It was just me, standing in my apartment, feeling more alive than I had since the mysterious headaches began.

No pain. No tears. No double vision.

Just me.

The corners of my lips lifted up in a triumphant smile and a laugh exploded from my mouth. It felt good to laugh again. I pumped my fist in the air and spun around in a wide circle, relishing the fact that I didn't want to fall back into the sweet embrace of sleep just to escape the torture being carried out on my skull.

"Thank God!" I yelled. "Thank you, thank you, thank you!"

After spending more hours in pain than I cared to count, I was no longer dreading the day, no longer cursing my existence and no longer asking God why he'd placed such a curse on my body. I could forget about the doctors that had turned me away and disregarded my symptoms. And on a brighter note, I didn't have to hate myself as I started my morning routine by self-medicating to the point of overdosing.

I could finally focus. Finally smile. Finally laugh.

The pain was *gone*.

Skipping from the kitchen to the living room, I spied the long neglected stereo remote.

*Oooh, yeah!*

I couldn't wait to sing at the top of my lungs until the neighbors complained. It had been too long since I'd been able to head-bang to my favorite death metal CD. Too long since I'd been able to dance, or jump from the furniture, or play air guitar until my arms grew weak. I was ready to act like a complete fool.

So, like a giddy schoolboy sneaking Ozzy records behind his parents' back, I reached for the remote, ready to enjoy the day.

But my hand came back empty.

"What the-"

I looked from my empty palm to the coffee table, where the remote remained undisturbed.

I reached for it again.

My eyes grew wide as I jerked back in surprise, confused when I didn't feel the hard plastic touch my skin. I wasn't sure if my eyes had grown so tired and unfocused because of so many hours spent in pain or if the morning light was somehow creating an optical illusion that I couldn't crack.

Either way, I reached for it one more time.

Gasping, I watched as my fingers slipped through the table, as if they were dipping through the glassy surface of a tranquil pond.

"What?"

I turned my hand back and forth in front of my face, inspecting the faulty limb. Was it me? My motor skills? My eyes? Something wasn't right. The line between my hand and my brain was short-circuiting somehow and I didn't know how to fix it.

Leaning forward, I attempted to rest my palm

against the marred surface of the table, but the wood didn't resist. It didn't hold my weight. It never moved beneath my touch. My hand floated freely, never coming into contact with anything, even though the table stood right there before my eyes.

I wasn't imagining it. It wasn't a hallucination or a projection. It was the same table I'd had for years, in the same place it had been since I moved into the apartment. But I couldn't touch it, couldn't feel it, couldn't move it. It just sat there, quietly mocking my inability to do something as simple as rap my fingers against the dark-stained wood.

*What in the hell is going on?*

Turning my attention away from the conundrum, I faced the rest of my apartment. Nothing had changed since I went to sleep the night before. The ugly floral wallpaper was still peeling off the walls, the sink still tapped out a steady rhythm from the drip I couldn't figure out how to fix, and the mismatched furniture was still as broken down and gaudy as it had always been.

Shaking my head, I gave up. I needed coffee. Lots and lots of coffee. Surely I'd be able to function with a little caffeine running through my system. I ventured around the small divider separating my bedroom from the rest of the apartment, intent on showering, getting dressed, and downing an entire pot of Folgers in order to start my day. But as soon as I stepped foot into my room, I stopped cold.

There, in my bed, was the covered figure of a person. If I hadn't known better, I would have sworn I'd gotten rip-roaring drunk the night before and had some company of the female variety. But that didn't

4

explain why I'd woken up on the kitchen floor instead of in my warm bed with someone's arm draped across my chest.

Padding my way across the floor, thankful that my socked feet didn't make a sound atop the well-worn carpet, I bent down to wake whoever was in my bed. I didn't want to frighten whoever was snoozing, but I did want to know *who* it was. Maybe it was someone I knew. Maybe a buddy had needed a place to crash. Or maybe it was a beautiful woman I didn't remember inviting over. Not that I'd ever invited a girl into my apartment before, but there's a first time for everything.

Softly clearing my throat, hoping I wouldn't startle the mysterious visitor, I nudged what I assumed was a foot beneath the covers. "Hello?" I said, barely above a whisper.

No movement. I tried again. "Excuse me, uh... person? Rise and shine. Time to get up."

My head fell back with an exasperated sigh as I realized that whoever it was, was a deep sleeper. Hoping that whoever it was didn't sleep in the nude, I made my way around the side of the bed where the covers were drawn back.

"Hey, buddy, can you-"

My entire body jolted to a stop as my words fell on deaf ears.

Or *dead* ears.

Wide, unblinking eyes stared into the nothingness behind me as I shook, as I fought for clarity, as I gazed down at the pale, lifeless skin of a man- a man I knew all too well. Clutching my chest, I stumbled away from his body. I was dreaming. I had to be. There was no other explanation.

  *RING*

  My head whipped toward the sound of my landline.

  "What the hell is going on?"

  *RING*

  My feet moved on their own, dragging my body across the room toward the blaring noise coming from my ancient phone.

  "Impossible. This... this is a prank or something. It has to be!"

  *RING*

  I reached the phone and instinctively grabbed for the handset. On contact, the already loud ring shot up to a high-pitched squeal, crackling and fuzzing like radio interference. I watched as the dial pad slipped through my trembling fingers again and again, eluding my touch just like the coffee table.

  *RING... BEEP*

  "Ryan, it's Quinn," my sister's worried voice boomed through the answering machine speaker. "I haven't heard from you in almost a week and it's really starting to freak me out. Call me back, please."

  "Quinn! No, I'm here! Don't hang up!"

  I tried to grab the phone again, but my fingers found no purchase. I may as well have been trying to hug a hologram. It was there. I could *see* it! But I couldn't feel it. I could barely feel my own hands.

  Panicking, I spun on my heel and turned to face all the things I'd acquired throughout my overly-materialistic life. Reaching for one thing after another, I tried to grab something, tried to touch, tried to feel. First a book, then a coffee mug, then onto my favorite

6

jacket, my empty wallet...

But my hands wouldn't cooperate. Everything I touched slipped through my fingers without moving even a fraction of an inch. My brain kicked into overdrive.

"What's happening?" I screamed as I thrust my hands into my hair and spun around the apartment, waiting for something to reach out and trip me, to wake me from this awful nightmare.

*KNOCK KNOCK KNOCK*

Jerking out of my panic, I sprinted toward the door. Something told me I wouldn't be able to answer it, but I had to try. Grabbing for the knob, I tried over and over again to wrap my fingers around the brass orb, but the only thing that registered my touch was the door itself. I beat against the barrier, screaming in frustration, intent on tearing it down, but it didn't budge. It didn't even make a sound.

I prayed that whoever stood behind that door held the key to the answers I needed. I needed them to come inside, to acknowledge the lifeless pile of flesh and bones melting into my mattress. I needed them to see, to explain. Because that wasn't just any corpse wrapped in my four-hundred thread count sheets.

It was my truth.

"Mr. Callahan?" Alice Whitlock, my landlady, called out as she continued to pound on the door. "Ryan? You're sister just called. She's worried. Could you open the door, please? Ryan, are you in there?"

"Yes! Alice, I'm here, I'm right here! Can you come inside? Do you have your key?"

"Ryan, I'm coming in."

I stepped away from the door and braced

myself; legs shoulder width apart and hands fisted at my sides, waiting for Alice to wiggle her key into the lock and enter my apartment. I hadn't been able to make heads or tails of anything happening around me, but maybe she could. Maybe this was all a sick joke and she was there to deliver the punch line. Or maybe I was dreaming. Maybe I just needed to wake up.

Standing there, praying to God that what I feared wasn't true, I willed Mrs. Whitlock to meet my eyes. I was ready to smile, tell her how sorry I was for worrying her, and make up some lame excuse about oversleeping before sending her on her way. I was ready for her to nod and make a joke about lazy young men before pulling me into one of her famous hugs.

But that didn't happen.

Alice Whitlock stepped into my apartment and looked right through me. Her light blue eyes scanned the rooms, sweeping side to side, searching for my presence. Pushing the door closed behind her, she took another step and immediately scrunched up her nose.

"Ryan, what have you been doing in here?"

"Nothing! I haven't been doing anything!" I said. "Mrs. Whitlock? Alice? Hello? Can you see me? I'm here. I'm right freaking here!"

I waved my hands around the side of her face, but she didn't stop, and I felt like collapsing in on myself. She couldn't see me, couldn't hear me. Reaching out, I tried to touch her shoulder, but couldn't. I lunged for her, grasping at nothingness as I tried to keep her from walking into my bedroom, but my hands met empty, stagnant air.

As frustration built inside my chest, I felt as if I would explode at any moment. I was usually a laid back, go with the flow kind of guy, but none of this made sense! I was standing right beside her. I could see myself, hear myself, even touch myself. But she couldn't? The truth of the situation kept trying to reveal itself to me, but I refused to acknowledge it. I flat out refused.

"Ryan?" Alice marched straight to the bed, and something deep inside me, deep in my soul, told me that her world, as well as mine, was about to be shattered. "Ryan, sweetie, time to wake up. Your sister is worried si-"

I stopped a few feet away, wringing my hands as I watched Mrs. Whitlock reach down and softly shake the arm of the body laying in my bed.

"Ryan?"

An uneasy air filled the room as she straightened her spine and a sharp gasp pierced her lungs. I could hear her fighting for breath as a weathered hand flew to her mouth and her shoulders began to shake. Instinct told me to go to her, to comfort her, to wrap my arms around her tiny frame, smooth down her silver hair, and assure her that everything was going to be okay.

But I couldn't. And it wasn't.

Feeling completely lost, helpless, and more alone than I'd ever been in my entire life, I dropped to my knees as I watched poor Alice Whitlock scream and run for the door.

# Mercy

Every single one of my earthly possessions fit neatly in the trunk and back seat of my beat up Ford Taurus with room to spare. It was a depressing sight.

"I can't believe you're really leaving us," my mother said as she followed me out the front door. "First Lyric and now you. What am I going to do with both of you gone?"

I would have answered, 'get a hobby', but that's really all my mother had. Hobbies. Organic gardening, tapestry weaving, tarot card reading, aura cleansing, rock painting, bead stringing... the woman was one walking hobby.

My parents, Gwen and Patterson Hunter, were what you could call 'born again hippies'. Throughout high school, they'd done their fair share of recreational drugs, read banned books, and had stood up to 'the man' in the form of unorganized protests and flat out violent riots. But once the real world came-a-callin', they both found themselves behind a desk, neck-deep in the corporate world.

That was until my older brother Lyric came along. Once they witnessed the miracle of childbirth, something in them sparked back to life. But instead of just taking things down a few notches and appreciating all life had to offer like any sane person would do, they went the extremist route and reverted back to their patchouli wearing, hemp t-shirt making, save the whales screaming former selves. Which was all well and great for them, but I'd be lying if I said my childhood hadn't been affected by their alternative lifestyle. After all, who names their children Lyric and Mercy? People who intentionally plant seeds of adversity in their children thinking it will somehow make them stronger adults, that's who.

"Are you sure you want to go?" My father asked as he pushed his horn-rimmed glasses up his nose. "Chicago's an awfully violent city. That can't be good for someone with such an absorbent soul, like you."

Absorbent soul? Like my innards were made out of Bounty paper towels?

Of course, in true Hunter fashion, my mother and father had waited until the last second to try and talk me out of my move. Up until I actually started packing the car, they'd spent months assuring me that my trip to Chicago was some kind of 'spirit journey'. But they couldn't have been more wrong.

For one, it wasn't a 'trip'. I was *moving* to Chicago. Moving, and I didn't plan on coming back. And two, I didn't want a journey, spirit or otherwise. I wanted roots- deep roots that could never be eradicated from the soil of my choosing. But my parents would never understand that and I didn't have the heart to tell them that living in a constant state of gypsy-like flux was raging hell on my 'absorbent soul'.

"Dad, Chicago is one of the most beautiful cities in the U.S. There are a million things to do there, a million things to see, and it's the only place I want to be right now. Oh, and stop talking about the crime rate. I too know how to do research, and guess what? Chicago is nowhere near as bad as you've made it out to be. So, nice try, but I'm going."

"The statistics for home invasion and armed robberies are through the roof," he pointed out.

"Yeah, there and in every other big city across the globe."

There was no talking me out of leaving, so they may as well have saved their breath. After living a life of no structure, zero stability, and nonexistent parental guidance, I was finally leaving the nest. Finally setting myself free.

Drew Gibbs, one of the few friends I'd managed to make over the years I'd spent jumping from one school to another, contacted me three days before graduation and blathered on and on about how great his new life in Chicago was turning out to be. That was all I needed to hear. I packed my things and counted down the days until I could hit the road and never look back.

I loved my mother and father dearly, but sometimes the life your parents surround you with isn't the life you're meant to live. Sometimes, your values, morals, and beliefs just don't match up to those of the people who breathed life into you. It's sad, especially when you're raised to believe that

12

families are a unit -one entity comprised of separate limbs, all operating on their own while still contributing to the closeness and well-being of the clan you were destined to be a part of- but I never felt like I belonged.

There had always been an enormous, invisible barrier between me and the rest of my family. It was obvious that they were one type of people, and I was another. I wasn't meant to live their life, and they wouldn't be all that accepting of what I had planned for mine.

"Are you sure you have everything?" My mother asked, sweeping her eyes over the boxes in my back seat.

"Yup, this is it." I held my arms open wide like Vanna White, showcasing my less-than-steller automobile.

"And you'll call when you get there?" She asked, her voice growing more urgent as I situated myself behind the steering wheel. "Is there a payphone close to where you'll be staying? Do you have enough change? Wait, I'll get you some quarters!"

"Mom!" I grabbed her before she had a chance to run inside for her Crown Royal bottle filled to the brim with loose change. "I have quarters, it's fine. I'll be fine. Promise. And yes, I'll call as soon as I get there."

"And this *friend* you're staying with, is he an alright guy?" My father leaned in my passenger side window and fiddled absentmindedly with the knob on the glove compartment.

"Well, he's not an axe murderer, if that's what

you mean." At my father's narrowed eyes, I sighed and addressed him without sarcasm. "Drew's a good guy, dad. And I have no romantic interest in him whatsoever, if that's what you're worried about."

"Oh, sweetie, we wouldn't care even if you did," my mom chimed in, "just as long as he's good to our little girl, that's all that matters. Right, Patterson? We're fine with it."

After pinching the bridge of his nose, shaking his head, and letting out one overly-dramatic sigh, my father nodded his head reluctantly. "Of course. Totally fine with it."

That was the most concerned my father had ever sounded about anything in my entire life, which was surprising, considering he was more flippant than anything when it came to his children.

"Don't worry, dad. It's not like that. Drew's a friend. End of story."

My mother ducked inside the car before I could shut the door. As she wrapped her arms around me, I had to swipe at my face to avoid getting a mouthful of her unruly, waist-length brown hair.

"You don't have to explain anything to us, Mercy. This is *your* adventure." She pulled back to look me in the eyes. "It's *your* life. If you want to experiment with this Drew guy, feel free. You should really take this time away to discover your body, your desires, your spiritual energy and what you like to-"

"Mom! Stop!" I pulled out of her hug and nearly swung the car door shut on her head in my haste to get away. "We are so not going down that road. Now is not the time for that particular discussion."

14

"Well, I think it's the perfect time actually." She leaned in through the open window and I wanted nothing more than to start the car and drive away right that second.

"You know, I'm not going to Chicago to work my way through a slough of guys, or to connect with my inner spirit child, or travel to another plane of existence via psychedelic drugs, okay? That's not what me leaving is about, and if you wish that for me or think that's what I'll be doing, then you don't know me at all."

"Mercy, I think your mother is just trying to tell you that it's okay for you to do all those things. It's a part of growing up, of learning who you really are and what you want out of life. There's no shame in any of it. Even if it does give your father indigestion just thinking about it."

Funny. It took my father eighteen years to finally start *acting* like a father. All those years of wishing my dad would set boundaries or at least *act* like he was worried about what his children were doing, and now, when I really wanted him to back off, he was layering it on thick.

I bit my tongue. Hard.

They were impossible, and perhaps slightly insane. My parents weren't warning me about the dangers of sex, drugs, and rock and roll. Instead, they were actually encouraging me to find and follow their footsteps all along the highway to hell.

It took everything in me not to tell them that I was different. That I was repulsed by their lifestyle and the choices they'd made. If my parents knew that I secretly wished they hadn't slipped off the corporate bandwagon and into the crazed life of middle-aged hippiedom, they'd be crushed.

Praying for some semblance of control, I squeezed my hands around the steering wheel so tightly my knuckles turned white. All I had to do was tell them I loved them, start the car, and leave. That was the plan.

But us Hunters have never been good at sticking to plans. So, without sparing a single thought about the consequences or repercussions of my words, I opened my mouth and let it fly.

"Look, all of that is great for you two, but that's your life, not mine. You don't see any shame in it, but I do. I'm tired of feeling like a freak. I want to be *normal*. I want a permanent address, and a normal job, and friends that don't care what color my aura is."

"Mercy!" My mother cried, as if the notion of me wanting something different had never crossed her mind.

"I'm tired of pretending to fit into this life, when it's clear that I don't."

"You're our daughter," my father said, "you've always fit into this life, into this family, whether you care to admit it or not."

"No, I don't." I buckled my seat belt and started the car. "My childhood was a joke, dad. When I was a kid, I wanted to do ballet but you said no. So while other little girls were going to recitals, I was taking part in your drugged up drum circles. And then in high school, I said I wanted to join the swim team. But instead of just signing the freaking form, you sent me to Florida for the summer to work in a turtle release program. Your whole attempt at parenting has

16

been completely ridiculous. I've told you time and time again what I want and what kind of a person I want to be, but you've never bothered to actually *listen.* And up until now, I've lived my life how you wanted me to with zero arguments. But now... I need to leave. I need to get out of here and go after the kind of life I've always wanted. A *normal* life."

Every time I spoke the word 'normal', my parents visibly flinched. In their house, under their rule, saying 'normal' was the equivalent of taking the Lord's name in vain or spitting on a statue of Buddha. It just wasn't done.

"I love you guys, I really do," I made an effort to infuse my voice with a little more compassion than I was feeling, "but you always encouraged me to be a free spirit. So that's what I'm doing."

My father scoffed and I turned to meet his eyes, daring him to say something, to try and prolong the argument.

He didn't.

"What you two fail to understand is that there are other ways to be free. It's not all organic clothing, peace riots -which is an oxymoron by the way- and fighting 'the man'. That doesn't seem too free to me. In all honesty, it's been exhausting trying to keep up with you two."

"So, this is you rebelling against us?" My mother asked, tears brimming at the corners of her eyes.

"No, mom. This isn't me rebelling," I said softly. "It's me showing you that there are a million different ways to be free, and I'm going out to find them."

My parents, in all their tie-died, bohemian wrapped, dreadlocked glory... looked so lost.

So, without another word, I blew them both a kiss, shifted my car into drive, and drove away.

# Chapter Two

# Ryan

"No! Get out! I'm not ready! I'm not dead! I'm right here!"

Screaming was getting me nowhere. I'd spent the better part of an hour following the police, the emergency personnel, and the coroner around the apartment, yelling as I wove in between their busy bodies, waving my hands around like a maniac, trying to get someone to just *see* me. I had to be seen. Had to be heard.

I didn't believe in ghosts or angels or anything of the sort, and I didn't put much stock into the afterlife. I always believed that when you die, you just disappear. The universe swallows you whole and you live on only in the hearts and minds of the people who truly loved you- if you were lucky enough to be loved. But as I watched the coroner console Mrs.

Whitlock, it was glaringly obvious I'd made a colossal mistake.

"What happened to him?" She asked.

The coroner, a man in his late fifties with a beer belly and hair implants, shrugged as he zipped up the body bag containing my stiff corpse. "Hard to say, ma'am, but my bet's on either heart attack or aneurysm."

"Heart attack?" Mrs. Whitlock's hand fluttered over her mouth. "But he was so young."

"You know kids these days. No sleep, too much stress, always on the go. It's not as uncommon as it used to be."

"I'm only twenty-one!" I yelled in his face before trying and failing to slam my hand against the gurney separating him from my beloved landlady. "People my age don't just croak in their sleep!"

"If you'd like, I can contact you once I get the results of the autopsy."

"Yes, yes please. I'd like that. He was such a sweet boy," Mrs. Whitlock glanced around the room before her eyes settled on the phone. "His sister called me, asked me to check up on him. Should... should I call her?"

My anger deflated at the thought of how Quinn would take the news. I'd never been close to my parents, but my twin sister was everything to me. I wasn't at all surprised that she'd been the one to call Mrs. Whitlock in the first place. She was one of the only people on earth who truly cared about my well-being.

My heart shattered for her. Quinn was alone now with no one to lean on. My parents would be distraught, but not like Quinn. They would grieve over the loss of their only son just as any other parent would, but she would no longer be in possession of that secret vibe, that mysterious twin connection we'd shared since birth. We were two halves of a whole and her lesser half had just been stripped away. In all honesty, even though I was dead and the life I'd lived had come to an end, I felt the same way.

"I'm sorry, Quinn. I'm so sorry."

As my apartment began to empty and they carried my body out the door, I moved away from all the commotion and settled for standing at the window, staring down at the hustle and bustle I'd never again be a part of. People were rushing along the sidewalk, going about their lives, not sparing a second's thought to the fact that everything could end when they closed their eyes.

I sure as hell hadn't been thinking about death when I rested my head on my pillow in my last night of life. I wasn't thinking about much of anything when I placed my glasses on my night stand, took a painkiller, and shut my eyes. Even though I'd been dealing with unexplained cranial pain for weeks, it never occurred to me that the reaper was waiting just around the corner, ready to take me away from everything I loved.

When the traffic on the sidewalk below began to dwindle, I looked back to find the apartment empty. I half expected the police to tear my place apart, looking for signs of foul play, but they hadn't. Every material possession I owned was still sitting where I left it.

As I looked around at what my life had

amounted to, a dull ache set up shop in my chest. It was more a metaphorical pain than a real pain, seeing as how I was dead and had no working nerve receptors, but it still felt as if my chest could cave in at any second from grief alone.

Did I resent the person I was and how I lived my life? Yes. But that wasn't what spawned the ache. No. The thought of someone coming in and boxing up my things was even more dismal than the realization that I couldn't do it myself because I no longer inhabited the same space as the breathing. That thought was so painful and consuming because I knew that person would be Quinn. And it would shred her heart to pieces.

Turning back to the window, I spent hours watching the sun set over the glistening buildings of blustery Chicago. With each passing second, the reality of death began to sink in.

There was no going back. Everything I'd done with my life was all I'd ever get to do. I wasn't getting a second chance to make things right, to be a better person. I was who I was and every imprint I'd made on my family, my friends, the world... it was all I had left. And soon enough, that would be gone as well. Just like the night sky erasing all traces of daylight. I too would soon fade away and be nothing but a distant memory.

I closed my eyes as the last sliver of sunlight fell beneath the horizon. For once in my life, I wished I could cry. I'd never been much of a crier, but I had nothing left, no way to grieve for myself, to grieve for my family, to grieve for the endless possibilities that had just been tossed in the dumpster. The need to shed tears was nearly unbearable as I stood in my quiet apartment, unsure of what to do with myself.

If a grand afterlife did exist, then why wasn't I being greeted by a warm, white light? Why were there no angels beckoning to me from the pearly gates? Why was I still in my crappy, run down apartment, completely alone and terrified of what was to come?

The answer hit me like a slap in the face.

"Because I'm dead... and I did nothing to deserve anything better than this."

# Mercy

The office building Drew worked in was easy enough to find. My sense of direction sucked, but at least I'd been smart enough to buy a GPS before leaving Indiana. My parents hated technology, so I'd had to hide it in a shoebox until I pulled out of the driveway, but it was a godsend.

Chicago traffic was unbearable, especially to an inexperienced driver like myself, but I arrived at my destination and breathed a sigh of relief as I cut the engine and stepped from the car. Craning my neck, I looked up and up, gawking at the intimidating structure like a tourist, but I couldn't help myself. It was massive. At least twenty stories. It would definitely take some getting used to if I got the job I was about to interview for.

Drew had been nice enough to put in a good word for me when he heard a spot in the mail room had opened up. Most young women fresh out of high school would balk at such a job. But not I. It was exactly the kind of position I'd hoped to find.

Easy. Tedious. *Normal.*

I took one deep breath after another before ascending the steps and pushing through the heavy glass door leading into the lobby. Everything about the place screamed uniformity. From the plain white tiles of the floor, to the polished granite desktops, to the clear glass and brushed nickle light fixtures hanging overhead. No bright colors. No creative vibe. No warmth at all. Even the air lacked definition.

*Perfect...*

I approached the main desk where a middle-aged man with a graying cowlick was busy hunting and pecking his way across a keyboard. His charcoal suit matched the décor perfectly and I thanked my lucky stars I'd thought to change before the interview.

Instead of my normal peasant skirt and tunic, I'd changed into a knee-length pencil skirt with a white, ruffled blouse. I'd never worn anything like it before, but I'd spotted it the second I walked through the doors at Macy's and knew it would help me land a job.

"Excuse me," I waved at the man behind the desk and he stopped what he was doing, seemingly grateful for the distraction.

"What can I do for you, dear?" His voice was deep and heavily laden with what seemed to be a French accent, but his English was purposeful and clear.

"Care to point me in the direction of the mail room?"

"Of course." He pointed to the elevator bay. "Take that all the way down to the basement level. The receptionist down there can help you find whatever you're looking for."

"Thank you, sir." I waved and started toward the elevators with a nervous, yet determined march.

"My pleasure, madame."

I smoothed out my skirt as I waited for the numbers above the closed doors to reach the ground level. I'd never had a real job before, so I had no idea what to expect, and my nerves were eating away at my confidence. Forget butterflies in my stomach. I had chainsaw wielding pterodactyls flying around my gut.

Breathing deeply, I reminded myself that if this fell through, there were plenty of other jobs I could apply for. My theory was that if I went for full disclosure and was up front about all my strengths and weaknesses, they couldn't ask for more. I didn't see the need to talk up my attributes or feign modesty. As long as I was myself, I'd end up where I needed to be.

The elevator dinged and I pulled my shoulders back as the doors slid open.

"Mercy! You made it." Drew stepped out of the elevator and surprised me with a hug. "Hey, if you'll give me two seconds, I'll take you down to meet with Kayla."

Before I could answer, Drew took off at a slow jog across the lobby floor. Stopping in front of the main desk, he withdrew an envelope from his pocket and tossed it to one of the receptionists who thanked him with a wide smile.

After a friendly wave, he jogged right back and gave me yet another hug. "Wow, you haven't changed a bit. How was the drive?"

He didn't seem to find that as insulting as I did.

I was *trying* to change. Not that he could have possibly known that.

"It was okay. You haven't changed either. Except for that mountain-man beard you've got going on there."

He ran a hand along his jaw, as if he had to feel his beard to remind himself it was there.

"Hey, the ladies love it." He shrugged one shoulder before turning and following me into the elevator.

"I'll bet they do," I laughed, nervously fiddling with my skirt again.

Drew leaned in and nudged me with his elbow. "Relax. You look fine."

"You think so?" I wasn't normally one of those girls who fished for reassurance from a man, but I was completely out of my element and I knew Drew was a straight shooter.

"Well, aside from your posture. Who do you think you're interviewing with? Hitler?"

I snorted back a laugh as I relaxed my shoulders just an inch and let my spine fall back into it's usual resting place.

"Much better. Now you look more like a human and less like an Autobot."

"You're doing wonders for my confidence right now," I said.

"You'll do fine. Just don't try to read her palm or tell her how to dread her hair or anything like that." Drew chuckled and I playfully elbowed him in the ribs.

"Jerk."

Of course, Drew knew about my complicated

relationship with my parents. We'd been pen pals ever since eighth grade and somehow over the years, we'd never lost contact. He was my confidant, and I his. He was one of the few people I knew who empathized with my situation. I mean, how could he not?

His mother still wore leopard print leggings she'd owned in the eighties and his father had no issue with informing strangers that he and his wife liked to 'experiment'. Needless to say, his parents had made his life just as difficult as my parents made mine.

"Any last minute advice?"

"Just be yourself," Drew said with a warm smile.

"Any *helpful* advice?"

He brushed his fingers through his beard thoughtfully before shaking his head. "Nope. I got nothin'. But whether you get the job or not, my couch is still yours for the foreseeable future."

"Thanks, Drew. And as soon as I score a job, I'll be out of your hair. I promise. I still have a hefty chunk of my graduation money left over, so that'll cushion me until I start getting regular paychecks."

"Got this all planned out, don't you?"

"Every step," I answered.

The elevator doors opened and Drew ushered me out into a drab, fluorescent-lit hallway lined with open doors. People rushed in and out, clutching paper tubes and envelopes to their chests, barking orders and requests into cell phones, and juggling packages, car keys, and disposable coffee cups.

It was exactly the kind of chaos I'd been dreaming of. Now, all I had to do was land the job.

Kayla Turner, the woman who interviewed me, was a saint in my eyes. After only talking with her for a maximum of five minutes, she offered me the job and I gladly accepted. Drew and I had done an incredibly embarrassing happy dance in the elevator and he clocked out for the day to take me out to celebrate.

While I fought to contain my squeals of excitement, I followed him through the streets of Chicago, bound for a restaurant in Chinatown that Drew swore up and down was the most authentic place to eat if you wanted real Asian cuisine.

"I can't believe it! That was so easy."

Drew shook his head as a warm smile graced his face. "Well, it's a mail room job, Mercy. It's not like you were interviewing to be CEO or anything."

"I know, but still! I can't believe I have a job. In Chicago! In a building that could fit the entire population of every commune I've ever visited with room to spare! I'm freaking out!"

Drew laughed. "Maybe you should dial down the excitement a few degrees. You haven't even started yet. You might hate it, God knows I do. It's monotonous, boring, the same crap day after day."

"It's perfect," I argued.

"We'll see if you still think that after delivering mail to sixteen floors of ungrateful office hags."

Drew didn't seem to grasp the fact that boring, monotonous work was what I had set out to find. Normality was something I'd always aspired to accomplish, and this move, this job, was my first step in that direction. In that interview I hadn't been 'the strange hippie girl'. I'd simply been 'that unemployed girl'. And now... I was 'that girl with a freakin' awesome job'.

I followed Drew through a beautifully constructed red archway boasting the words *Welcome to Chinatown* in gleaming gold letters. All around us, people of all ethnicities scurried about as they chatted on cell phones, bobbed their heads to whatever was playing through their earbuds, or held hands with children as they perused all the ornately crafted trinkets the specialty shops had to offer. It was a charming atmosphere.

Most of the signs sported Chinese characters in big, bold script with an English translation below. Squinting my eyes, trying to make out as much as I could, a certain sign caught my eye and I slapped Drew on the arm in excitement.

"Look! Vacancy ahead! Let's go check it out."

Before he could agree, I pulled him in the direction of the arrow on the sign and down a side street until we stood in front of a redbrick building labeled 'Chinatown Apartments'.

"Oh, this used to be a motel," he said. "Someone bought it last year and renovated it into apartments."

"Spend a lot of time in Chinatown, do you? You sure are in the know."

"Best food in town, I'm tellin' ya. C'mon, I'm starving." He pulled me back toward the main street, intent on finding sustenance.

"Okay, but can we go back after we eat? I really want to check it out."

"You want to live in Chinatown?" He asked,

sparing me a glance over his shoulder.

"Sure," I shrugged. "Seems like a nice enough place."

"Yeah, if you want all your belongings to smell like egg rolls forever."

"Hey, there are worse smells," I laughed.

"Isn't that the truth. Hey, right here," Drew stopped and pulled me into a crowded but relaxed restaurant. "The Mayflower. Best Chinese food in all of Chicago."

Despite having complete faith in Drew's taste in cuisine, I was weary. Before we'd even made it into the main dining area, we passed a tank filled with murky water where a half dozen soft shelled turtles congregated in a bare corner. I would have just wrinkled my nose and scoffed at the way they treated their animals, if it hadn't been for the sign advertising 'Fresh Seafood Daily'. Realizing that the turtles were items on the menu instead of pets made me feel even worse. Both for the turtles and the patrons.

"Are you still a vegetarian?" Drew asked as a hostess escorted us to a table.

"Last I checked, yes."

As much as I wanted to change, the idea of eating meat still repulsed me. There are just some things your parents instill in you that you can't escape no matter how hard you try. And even if I had a craving for an eight ounce ribeye steak, I knew the likelihood of my stomach being able to digest that was nil.

"Well, you're in luck. Half their menu consists of veggie dishes."

I took my menu from the hostess and thanked

her before she cracked a small, polite smile and scurried away. Judging from the way she avoided eye contact with the majority of customers, I guessed that English wasn't her first language, if it was one of her languages at all.

"Real, authentic Chinese food, huh?"

"The best. So, what are we in the mood for? Soup? Pasta? The dried and fried remains of our little soft shelled friends out front?"

"Absolutely not!"

I was already gearing up to tell Drew the top ten reasons why eating turtle was bad for humans as well as the ecosystem, but he held his hands up in surrender before I could begin my tirade.

"Kidding. Our little reptile friends are safe. For now. How's... mushroom soup sound?"

I did a quick search of the menu to see if there was anything else that sounded appetizing. There wasn't.

"Sounds great."

After a few short minutes, a young Asian girl that couldn't have been more than fifteen came to take our orders. Her English was only slightly accented, so it was easy enough to understand. For me at least. Drew still had to stare at her mouth while she was talking, like a deaf person reading lips, and even then she had to repeat every word.

After she was gone, he lifted his glass of water and I followed suit.

"To new beginnings," he said.

"Even though that's the most cliché thing I've heard all day, I'll drink to it."

"I'm a walking cliché, baby. Tall, dark, and-"

"Conceited."

Drew feigned outrage and I couldn't help but laugh. If there was one thing Drew *wasn't*, it was conceited, and we both knew that. He was the most down to earth, modest, and easy-going person I'd met in all my years hopping from school to school. It's why I treasured his friendship so much.

Looking back, if I could have picked the person I fell in love with, it would have been Drew. No contest. But I couldn't be romantically involved with him. The biggest reason being that there was no spark between us. None whatsoever. Never had been. Not even an electric blankets worth of heat passed between us. So, we settled for being friends, and that was more than enough.

# Chapter Three

## Ryan

Days passed and I impatiently waited for Quinn to come pack up my belongings. To my surprise, however, Mrs. Whitlock did it herself. Alice must have let hundreds of tears spill down her cheeks as she packed up my clothes, books, movies, and dishes. When she got to my computer, she was extra careful, and I loved her for that. She knew exactly what that expensive piece of machinery housed- my life's work. There was no telling how many articles, manuscripts, screenplays, and every other kind of unpublished drivel that floated around that hard drive, never to be read, never to be put out into the world.

"I'm sorry, Alice," I said, even though I knew she couldn't hear me. "I'm sorry you have do this."

She worked through the afternoon, until her hands began to shake and it became difficult for her to haul boxes down to the storage shed. With her last drop of energy, she threw my remaining things into a trash bag, lugged it out into the hall, and asked another tenant to help carry it downstairs. Once that was dealt with, my home was void of everything except what had been there when I arrived over a year ago.

Alice, bless her soul, wiped her tears, glanced around the apartment one last time, and blew a kiss into the air before shutting and locking the door behind her. As I listened to her descend the stairs, I bid her farewell and turned to face the night alone.

Forever alone.


Not having the ability to sleep is something I was sure I'd never get used to. Humans are creatures of habit, so when the sky turned dark, my instinct was to crawl into bed, close my eyes, and turn in for the night. But the dead don't sleep. Or eat. Or breathe.

Obviously...

I didn't know what to do with myself. Death was beginning to seem like one long, never-ending bout of insomnia, and I feared I would have to spend eternity locked away in a vault of my own thoughts, my own regrets, and my own insecurities. My death didn't bring me peace, as I once expected it would. It was quite the opposite, really. I was plagued with a profound sense of unease.

That night, I forced myself to reminisce over every detail of my life. Every fault. Every what-if. Every road not taken. But scattered through those depressing thoughts were memories of things I would miss. Visiting with my sister. Hanging out with friends from high school. Geeking out at the Field Museum of Natural History every other weekend... All trivial things, but things I'd miss nonetheless.

By the time the sun began to rise and the streets below began to fill with morning joggers and singles doing the walk of shame, I had lost myself. I wasn't sure who I was or who I had been.

For as long as I could remember, I'd had a very specific vision of what I wanted to do and who I wanted to be. I based everything I was on that vision. The plan was to get my foot in the door career wise, rock the publishing world, and then, finally, start a family. I wasn't a workaholic like my parents, so I knew I wanted a wife and children more than I wanted to be successful. I wanted to be surrounded by people who I loved, who loved me back, and who filled my heart to the brim with happiness.

But now, that vision was nothing more than an unattainable fantasy.

Every possibility of happiness had been ripped from my hands, stolen from my heart, and crushed under the heavy, unyielding foot of mortality.

"God, this is depressing."

"I'll say. You've been staring out that window for hours."

"GAH!"

I whirled around, clutching at my chest, eyes flying wide as I realized I wasn't alone.

There, sitting on the arm of the couch, was a little girl. She couldn't have been more than seven or eight years old, but there was something about her, something that immediately set me on edge. She radiated a certain kind of energy and a prickling sensation at the back of my neck told me I was in the presence of something special. Something profound. Something... ethereal.

"You- you can see me?"

"Of course I can see you, silly. You're standing right there."

Her voice was a tinny soprano, like that of many young girls, but beneath her soft words was something more, something indescribable. A natural white noise, much like waves crashing onto a sandy shore, or wind blowing through the thin leaves of a mimosa tree. It was unsettling, but only because it was so foreign. I *felt* like it should put me at ease, but it didn't.

"Who are you? What are you doing here? Are you- are you alive?" I approached her as I fired off one question after another, wanting -no, needing- to know who she was, where she came from, and what she was doing in my apartment.

But instead of answering any of my questions she continued to swing her feet off the edge of the couch. She stared at me with wide, hazel eyes as her feet worked back and forth.

Back and forth.

Back and forth.

"Who are you?!" I screamed when she made no move to answer my questions.

My harsh tone simply rolled off her shoulders. She wasn't the tiniest bit phased. Instead, she put one tiny finger to her lips and closed her eyes.

"Shh," she said, "I love this song."

I tilted my head to the side, listening for whatever she was hearing, but only the sounds of traffic and garbled voices from the street below registered in my ear.

"But there's no music."

"Shh," she repeated, never opening her eyes as she began to hum an eerily familiar tune. I couldn't place it, but I knew I'd heard it somewhere before. Which unnerved me further.

"Seriously. Who the hell are you and why are you here?" I practically sobbed the words, forgoing the intensity and anger I'd felt the first go-round. "Tell me, please!"

More humming.

Overwhelmed, and more than a little terrified of the little anomaly invading my living room, I charged across the room and grabbed for her arm.

Bad idea.

A spark of electricity so strong, so blinding, so extreme, sent me scrambling out of the room. I shook out my extremities, assessing the damage the little monster had just inflicted on me, but I was fine. Well, aside from being dead, I was completely intact. I turned, ready to rip into her, but she was gone.

The couch was empty.

"What the-?"

I thought for a moment that I had imagined the whole thing. After all, my living room was empty. I turned to the bedroom. She wasn't in there either. I whirled around to inspect the kitchen.

My breath caught at the sight of her perched atop the kitchen counter.

"Don't you have any manners?" She yelled as her hazel eyes turned on me. "You can't just waltz up and touch people whenever you feel like it! What's the matter with you?"

"I- I'm sorry. You just seemed so... alive. Are you real?"

"I'm sittin' here, aren't I?" She snapped.

"Technically. I guess. But I'm standing here, too. Doesn't mean I'm real."

In a movement too fast for my eyes to track, she flickered across the floor and perched herself on the window sill.

"Just because you're not alive, doesn't make you any less real."

I followed her but kept my distance. Whatever happened when I touched her before, I didn't want that to happen again. Ever. It wasn't painful, just overwhelming. And I'd had my fill of being overwhelmed.

"Pretty sure you're wrong. I'm dead, therefore, I don't exist. Therefore, I'm not real. I'm a shadow of what I used to be."

"Are you saying shadows aren't real?" She countered.

"No, they're real. Just, not concrete."

"Ah, so anything abstract isn't real? Pain. Love. Forgiveness. Happiness. Those are all abstract things. You can't see them, can't feel them. Does that make them any less real?"

I opened my mouth to answer, only to realize I'd been had. By a child.

"Smart," I mused. "How old are you anyway?"

She sighed as she flipped her wavy brunette hair over one shoulder and began to braid it with her tiny, agile hands. "I don't have an age, per se."

"Per se?" I laughed. "You're an awfully sharp

little girl."

She let go of her hair and focused her dark eyes directly on mine. "You could say that."

With those four words, her presence hit me like a ton of bricks and I realized she had the answers I'd been desperately searching for. She held the key, *my* key, to the afterlife. I hoped.

"Why are we here?" I asked.

She glanced around at the empty walls and shrugged. "Where else should we be?"

"No, I mean, why are we here at all. I thought when you died you were supposed to go to Heaven or something."

A knowing smile stretched across her tiny mouth. "Well, I guess we're in 'something' then."

Okay, so maybe she didn't have all the answers. At least, if she did, she didn't feel like sharing.

"Then shouldn't we be leaving? Shouldn't we be *going* to Heaven?"

She threw her head back in laughter, one of those laughs that tells you the person is laughing *at* you, not *with* you.

When she regained her composure, she turned back to me with soft, yet omniscient eyes.

"Oh boy, you've got a lot to learn."

I didn't understand. I couldn't even begin to wrap my brain around what she was saying, what she was, or why she was there. All I knew was that I needed her. But at the same time there was a voice, a voice that didn't belong to either of us, that whispered an important secret.

*She needs you...*

I approached the window and stood with her as we watched the city below come to life. I didn't understand anything that was happening around me, but I knew one day I would. And one day could wait. Patience wasn't something I was blessed with in life, but in death, I knew it was something I'd have to learn. There were no deadlines, no ticking clock, no race to the finish line. I had all the time in the world. It was... freeing.

"What's your name?" I asked.

Turning to me, the beautiful little girl opened her mouth in a full, wide, mesmerizing smile that completely disarmed me as she spoke with the delicacy of a thousand singing angels.

"Willa."

# Mercy

There was one thing about Chicago I was sure I'd never get used to. The entire town smelled of raw sewage. All. The. Time. Every now and then, I'd get a whiff of exhaust fumes or sulfur, but for the most part, it reeked of urine and feces.

"Disgusting," I muttered to myself as I walked the few blocks between Drew's apartment and Chinatown.

I kept my head down, hoping the perfume sprayed across my blouse would mask the overwhelming scent trying its best to upset my stomach. For the first time since I'd left home, I wished my parents' patchouli oil had stuck to all my belongings. It was distinct, and often agitated my keen sense of smell, but I was sure it could drown out the disgusting scent of a city so well lived in.

Once I strolled through Chinatown Gate, the smell of dumplings and spring rolls slowly replaced the rank aroma the rest of Chicago wore like a badge of honor. The sidewalks were busy as they had been the night before but everyone seemed to have a sense of purpose, a sense of belonging I hadn't quite grasped just yet.

For once, being surrounded by hundreds of speed-walking strangers didn't bother me. On the contrary, it perked up my spirits. I wanted to be one of them. I wanted to be a permanent resident of the Windy City and have that same sense of certainty of those around me.

After entering through the gate, I turned right after Pui Tak Center and quickly found the redbrick building that housed the Chinatown Apartments. I took a deep, bracing breath and swung open the glass door.

I didn't speak a word of Chinese and feared that all the tenants, as well as the entire staff, would be of Asian decent and I wouldn't be able to get very far due to the language barrier. But luckily, the same woman who was manning the desk when I dropped off my application the night before was still there.

"Hello," I said cheerily. "I'm Mercy Hunter. I dropped off an application last night. I just wanted to come by and change some of my contact info."

After dinner at The Mayflower, Drew had taken me to get a cell phone. It was the first piece of modern technology I'd ever owned and I was on Cloud 9 learning the ins and outs of instant communication and social media. I immediately understood the draw of such luxuries, but I'd gotten it solely for work, emergencies, and so I'd have a contact number for people like the owner of the Chinatown Apartments to reach me if my application was ever approved.

"Yes, dear," the older lady replied with a friendly smile. "I have your application right here."

She flipped through a large stack of papers before retrieving one marked with a yellow post-it note. "Here you go."

I took the application, scribbled over Drew's number, and replaced it with my own before returning it to her.

The aging woman replaced it among what had to be at least one hundred other applications before turning her easy smile my way. She paused, taking a moment to assess my wardrobe.

I was wearing jean shorts, flip-flops, and a plain black t-shirt. All things I'd picked up the night before while Drew and I were out shopping. It was simple and unassuming. I loved it. It was a nice change from the colorful tunics and flowing skirts my parents had always insisted I wear.

"Got a job?" She asked, surprising me.

"Yes, ma'am. It's new, but I've got one."

"You smoke? Drink? Do drugs?"

"No, no, and no. I'm pretty boring," I laughed.

The laugh lines around her eyes crinkled, reminding me of my own grandmother who we'd lost my freshman year of high school. "Boring is good, dear. At least when it comes to my job."

She extended her hand and I shook it with gusto. "Alice Whitlock. Landlady."

"Mercy Hunter," I nodded toward the stack of applications. "But you already knew that."

She pulled her hand away and eyed me curiously. "Interesting name. What's your story?"

"My story?" I shrugged. In my opinion, I

hadn't lived long enough to really have a *story*. "Just moved here from Indiana, landed a job yesterday, now looking for a place to stay. That's about it."

"What part of Indiana?"

"North Vernon."

She wrinkled her nose. "Small town."

"You've been there?" I asked.

"I have a son who lives in Columbus, so I've heard of it."

"Well, It's nothing to write home about. I didn't live there long, but that's where my parents are for now."

"Are you going to school?"

"Uh, no, I just graduated high school and I'm taking some time off before I start looking at colleges."

She nodded. "Never a bad idea. So do you have a lot of friends in the city? A boyfriend, maybe?"

I chuckled. "No and no. Just my friend Drew and we're not dating or anything."

Alice Whitlock may have been tiny, but she was intimidating when she was in interrogation mode. She leaned back against the counter with a heavy sigh, as if just standing was exhausting.

"So, fresh out of high school, new job, no boyfriend."

When she put it that way, I sounded like the lamest person to ever inhabit the city of Chicago.

"Uh, yeah. That about sums me up."

She reached forward and slid my application off the top of the stack. Tapping a single finger to her chin, she scanned it in silence. I watched her eyes bounce back and forth across the page as she pursed

45

her lips to one side and then the other. Normally, I could tell what people were thinking by their body language, but Mrs. Whitlock seemed to be the exception.

I rocked back and forth on my heels, waiting for her to say something. Anything. I wanted to know where I stood and her continued silence unnerved me. Why was she picking apart the words I'd scrawled across my application? Was she considering me? Did she think I was a nutcase? Was she suspicious of my lack of references? I wasn't sure.

After over a minute had passed, she folded the sheet of paper, stuffed it in her back pocket and lifted her smiling eyes to my face.

"Guess what?" She asked.

"What?" I gripped the edge of the counter, excitement and nerves colliding in my belly.

Without verbally answering, she took the enormous stack of applications... and threw them in the trash.

I clapped my hands together as a squeal burst through my lips."Really?"

"When would you like to move in?"

"Uh, now?"

She rounded the counter, chuckling to herself, before threading her arm through mine and leading me toward the stairwell. "I'll show you where you'll be, have you sign some papers, and get you a set of keys."

"Oh, my gosh, thank you so much! Really, you have no idea how happy this makes me. I thought I'd have to apply to dozens of places before I found anything. This is perfect."

"Fond of dim sum, are you?" She laughed.

I had no idea what dim sum actually was, so I just nodded as an enormous grin plastered itself across my face.

There was no elevator in the building, so we walked the three flights of stairs up to the vacant apartment. I expected Mrs. Whitlock to be worn out by the stairs due to her age, but she wasn't even winded.

"This is you, right here," she said, gesturing to a door adorned with tarnished gold numbers. "Number thirty-three." She grabbed onto an enormous key-chain attached to her belt buckle by a carabiner and flipped through at least ten keys before arriving at the right one.

I waited in rapt suspense, trying my best not to bounce on the soles of my feet as she paused in unlocking the door.

"There are some things about this place that might make you uneasy," she said. "But I'd like for you to have a look around before we get into the gritty details."

I nodded, not caring about 'gritty details' because all I cared about was having a place of my own. I didn't care if the place had lead paint peeling off the walls or an army of cockroaches that moved my furniture around while I slept... I was getting that key.

The lock clicked and Mrs. Whitlock opened the door wide, gesturing for me to enter while she stayed in the hallway. I took one step inside and instantly went on alert.

The hair on the back of my neck stood on end

as goosebumps erupted down my arms and legs. The small apartment was easily twenty degrees colder than the world outside, which made no sense since it was late summer and the air conditioning unit wedged into the window wasn't even plugged in.

"It's... quiet," I whispered.

I couldn't very well tell Alice that the room was holding it's breath, even though that's exactly what it felt like to me. My first instinct was to call my parents, who were well versed in the art of cleansing homes by burning sandalwood and sage, but I abandoned that thought before it even had time to fully form. That was ridiculous. I didn't do those things anymore. The new Mercy was through meditating, through living her life jumping from ritual to ritual, and was saying goodbye to auras, chakras, and dharma once and for all.

Surely there was a perfectly reasonable explanation for the way my forehead broke out into a cold sweat, the way my heart beat a little faster, and the way the air in the room seemed to thicken and stew around me. But whatever the reason, I couldn't ignore the voice in my head that told me something was very, very off.

# Chapter Four

# Ryan

The wavy locks of her simple blonde pony tail swung back and forth as she walked through the door. Her blue eyes scanned the room, eagerly soaking up every detail even as her smile slowly began to slip with every step she took. And I was a goner.

She was beautiful.

Beautiful in a different way. Not in a way I was used to seeing. Every girl I'd ever dated was very well put together. Designer clothes, perfectly highlighted hair, simple gold jewelry, manicured nails- the works. This girl didn't seem put together at all, at least not in the same sense. She looked natural. Real. Uncomplicated.

She also looked terrified.

I took a step closer and she cringed away, as if she could feel my presence. Her action made me stop in my tracks and turn back to face Willa, who was smiling at the girl like they were old friends.

I took another step, which put me inches away from her, and I watched as the tiny blonde hairs at the base of her neck stood on end under her wild pony tail. Goosebumps sprung up along her skin, starting at her shoulders and moving all the way down to her hands. She stood stock-still, not breathing, not moving, just... listening?

*That's a little freaky.*

"Cold," she whispered to herself as she crossed her arms over her chest. She looked back to Mrs. Whitlock, who was still standing in the hallway wearing a tight smile. She refused to cross the threshold, and I didn't blame her. After all, she'd been the one to find my body. From the look on her face, I gathered that she would have rather boarded up the door than rent the place out just days after my death.

"Take a look around," she urged the newcomer. "Let me know what you think."

The blonde moved through the small space, inspecting the bedroom, the cramped bathroom, and the kitchenette. I followed her every move, trying to get a read on her, but it was impossible. Her mouth was pulled into a tight line, her breathing was controlled, and her rigid posture never wavered. Her movements were mechanical, as if she were aware of every joint and muscle and tendon and was keeping them all in check. She was *trying* to seem indifferent. But her eyes told another story.

She was scared.

But of what? I had no idea.

"Don't be creepy."

I turned to find Willa's hands planted firmly on her hips and her eyebrows drawn together, like a mother scolding an errant child.

"I'm not being creepy."

"Right. Because standing two millimeters away from a person and breathing down their neck when they can't see you is normal social etiquette."

"I don't breathe," I said, slapping a hand to my chest. "Dead, remember?"

"Irrelevant. Stop being weird."

She was right, of course, but there was something about this girl. She was *different.*

When Alice and the coroner had shown up to retrieve my body, I'd tried everything in my power to reach out to them, to let them know I was there. But now, I felt the need to hide. I watched her intense blue eyes rove over the place my body last rested and got the sense that she *knew.* And that knowledge snowballed until I was struck with an exciting yet terrifying impossibility: The beautiful stranger *looking* at me.

"I think I need to leave," I whispered to Willa as I backed away.

"You can't," she replied at the same volume. "And why are we whispering? She can't hear us."

The blonde's head twitched to the side as she stared off into space, her eyes narrowing in concentration.

"Are you sure about that?"

# Mercy

Mrs. Whitlock closed the door behind me and we walked back downstairs to the lobby. I thought it was weird that she hadn't stepped foot inside the apartment, but if she felt the same thing I did as I wandered through the quiet rooms, I didn't blame her.

"The young man who used to live there, his name was Ryan," she began quietly, taking a seat behind the counter. Her eyes grew sad, aging her a decade. "So polite, that boy. Always on time with rent, always quiet, never any kind of trouble. He'd even stop by for a chat if he saw me working the desk. We'd talk about the weather or our families or new places to eat around the city. He worked from home so he didn't get out a lot, but when he did he always made time to catch up. It really lifted this ole gal's spirits. It was just small talk, you know, but it meant a lot. I really cared for that young man."

"Why'd he leave?" I asked.

"He died."

"Oh, I'm so sorry."

"Aneurism, they said." She shook her head in disbelief. "Died in his sleep."

I'd be lying if I said the idea of someone dying in my new apartment didn't make me cringe. It did, but I tried to hide that calloused fact from Mrs. Whitlock. Unfortunately, she noticed.

"Don't worry, dear. The bed's been replaced."

That wasn't what worried me. What had me on edge was the fact that the stillness of the apartment now made perfect sense. The air reeked of sadness and loss. There was a certain shadow of restlessness that blanketed every surface the late Ryan had ever touched. And his touch still lingered. But I had to wonder if that was the only thing still lingering in the frigid living quarters.

"Having second thoughts?" Mrs. Whitlock asked with a raised brow.

"What? Oh, no. No, that doesn't bother me," I lied.

"Great." She reached out to pat my hand. "I'll go get the paperwork."

She moved around the corner and entered a small door labeled 'office' and I took a seat in one of the gaudy armchairs in the lobby. The location of the apartment was great, the rent would be easy to swing with my new job, and I'd already gone and fallen in love with all the ornate buildings and friendly people of Chinatown. I *wanted* to live there, and a slight case of heebie-jeebies wasn't going to stop me.

After I signed the rental agreement, handed over first and lasts months rent, received a set of keys, and thanked Mrs. Whitlock, I emerged outside with a renewed sense of purpose. My life in Chicago was beginning and the feeling of being tethered down by a job and a lease was invigorating, contrary to my parents' beliefs.

They aimed to be free in every sense of the word. They lived to be able to speed out of town at a moment's notice if they suddenly got an itch to visit friends in Berkeley. They never made plans to, but they always ended up at 'The Farm', which was a hippie commune in rural Tennessee, at least three or four times a year. And even though neither of them owned a calendar, they always managed to make it out to the Black Rock Desert in Nevada for Burning Man every September.

They were the very definition of 'fly by the seat of your pants'. But not me. They never did understand my need for structure, my burning need to grow to be a productive member of society, a society whose norms and customs they rejected.

Yes, I respected their pacifistic views on life, unity, and their reverence for the environment, but I wasn't sure how selling beaded curtains out of the back of a van and smoking enough marijuana to knock out a moose had anything to do with any of those ideals. Of course, they didn't see how working a regular nine-to-five job, wearing mass-produced clothing, or eating genetically modified food was the way to live either.

But that's what I wanted to do. That's the kind of person I wanted to be. And one day, I planned to prove to them that it wasn't all bad. Yes, I'd jump feet first into the corporate world. I would work a meaningless job for as long as I felt like it. But then, I'd start climbing. I had so many great ideas formulating in the back of my mind.

Maybe I could found an organization that helped the environment, or a non-profit that sent workers to third-world countries to help starving children. I could even make a sizable donation to a woman's shelter or children's hospital or rehabilitation clinic for animals; any place that really made a difference. And then they would see. They would understand that there are better ways, more effective ways, to help our world.

At Drew's, I gathered what little belongings I hadn't kept in my car, left him a note on the coffee table, and drove back to Chinatown to start my new life, in my new home. I parked behind the building in a lot reserved for tenants. Anywhere I needed to go in the city I could get to by walking or taking the L line, so I planned on selling my car since it would just be sitting there collecting dust.

I'd never ridden in an elevated train before, but I looked forward to the experience. Actually, there was a lot I was looking forward to doing in Chicago. The train, exploring the city, decorating my apartment, making friends at work, maybe meeting a guy- the possibilities were endless.

But before I started all of that, there was something very important I had to do. After parking the car, I took my cell phone out of my pocket and dialed the only number I knew by heart. My mother and father didn't own a phone, which was ridiculous, but I could leave a message at the house where my parents and half the neighborhood congregated every night for yoga, meditation, dinner, and God knows what else. I could get a message to them and let them know that I was fine. However much I disagreed with their lifestyle and hoped to escape it, they were still my parents, and I loved them. They didn't deserve to worry about me.

Nervously clutching the phone to my ear, I hoped I didn't have to speak to anyone I knew personally. I wasn't sure how my parents had taken my little parting speech and the thought of one of their friends giving me the what-for over the phone wasn't something I was looking forward to.

"Yellow?"

I smiled, instantly recognizing the deep voice on the other end.

"Lyric! What are you doing there? I thought you were still in Manitou Springs."

"Just got back this morning. Man, you should have been there, Mercy. It was beautiful."

"I don't doubt it."

My brother Lyric was six years older than me. He was also a nomad; a hippie without a home, without a commune, who traveled solo everywhere he went. Whereas my parents moved from place to place every year or so just out of boredom, Lyric moved every *week*, trekking from place to place for work, or just because 'the road called to him'.

I never understood how he lived out of the backseat of his car (which, like mine, wasn't insured) or how he managed to call home every weekend, even when he found himself in places like the Pine Barrens trying to snap a picture of the Jersey Devil or off the coast of South Carolina photographing a clutch of newly hatched Leatherback turtles emerging from the sand.

"Rainbow Falls was especially amazing. I'll have to show you my prints next time I see you."

"I'd love that," I said. "Um, is mom or dad around by any chance? I need to talk to one of them."

"I think mom's out in the yard with the kids, hang on, I'll get her."

"Thanks, bub."

A few moments later, my mother's voice was singing through the phone.

"Hi, sweetie! Why didn't you call sooner? We were worried about you."

"Sorry, mom." My shoulders relaxed as I realized she didn't sound angry or disappointed. "It's just been crazy getting situated here."

"Situated? What had to be situated? I thought you were staying with your friend."

And here came the hard part...

"I- I was. But I just sighed a lease for my own apartment today. Isn't that great?"

I held my breath, but was met with silence. After it became too much to bear, I barreled on, needing to get everything out in the open.

"And I start my new job at the beginning of the week. I'm working in a mail room. I think I'll really like it. Everyone in the building seems really nice. Drew got me the interview, actually. After I got the job, he took me out to eat at this really great restaurant in Chinatown just a short ways from where I'll be living." I waited. I could hear the children playing in the background so I knew the line hadn't gone dead. My mother was just trying to make heads or tails of the bomb I'd just dropped. "Mom? Say something, please."

Part of me wanted my mother to lay into me, to tell me how toxic paperwork and the corporate world could be. I wanted it because I expected it. But the other part of me... it wanted nothing more than for my mother to tell me she was happy for me and proud of me. I didn't think that was too much to ask.

"Mercy Earth-Echo Hunter," she sighed around my full name. "What am I going to tell your father?"

*Ah, there's the disappointment...*

My eyes fell closed as I shook my head. What did I have to do to make her come to grips with my decision? Strengthening my resolve, I refused to let her get to me.

By her reaction, you'd have thought I was calling home to tell her I was pregnant with a crack dealer's baby or that I needed bail money for robbing a liquor store. Actually, either of those things probably would have been easier for her to accept, which proved just how irrational she could be.

"Why don't you tell your husband that his little girl landed a really good job that she's looking forward to starting and a nice apartment in a good part of town. I know that's horrible, so try to soften the blow if you can." I laid the sarcasm on thick.

"Mercy, listen-"

I cut her off. "Tell him that I went out and bought an entire closets worth of work clothes made out of denim and polyester and wool and satin and a bunch of other synthetic materials that are bad for me. Tell him that I ate a bite of a hamburger just to know what it tasted like. Tell him that I bought a cell phone that will give me brain cancer and let the government keep tabs on me. Tell him all that and then cry over how big of a disappointment your daughter has become."

Without waiting for her response, I pulled the phone away from my ear and ended the call.

I took a deep, cleansing breath and leaned back against the heated metal of my beat-up car as I wondered why I couldn't just have *normal* parents. Parents that participated in the PTA, who went grocery shopping in chain stores, drank coffee and read the newspaper... who supported their kids in whatever they wanted to do in spite of how much it conflicted with their personal beliefs. I wasn't sure if parents like that even existed. I hoped they did and I vowed that I would *be* that kind of parent if I ever had children.

My phone startled me as it began buzzing in my hand. I jerked the screen to my face, recognizing the number calling in.

"Hello."

"You're breaking their hearts, Mercy. You know that, right?"

Exhaling a ragged breath, I started pacing the length of my car. "You know, Lyric, it's not as if I'm trying to. We just have very conflicting ideas when it comes to how and where I should live my life. And I'm sorry if that breaks their hearts but I can't think about their hearts right now, not while I'm busy trying to follow mine."

Lyric cursed under his breath as the sound of someone playing a didgeridoo bellowed out in the background, making it hard for us to hear each other.

"Can you still hear me?" He asked. "Mercy, you there?"

"Yeah. I'm here."

He said something else, but I couldn't make out the words.

"Look, I've gotta go, Lyric. I have stuff to unpack."

"Okay, sis," he yelled. "Just, uh... I love you, okay?"

"I love you, too."

"Stay safe."

"Always. Bye."

The phone went dead and I shoved it back in my pocket. Even though I still felt bad about my parents' disappointment, hearing Lyric's voice and telling him I loved him somehow made me feel better. I may have been the world's worst daughter, but maybe I was only runner up when it came to the world's worst sister.

Vowing not to let their opinions bother me, I grabbed a box from my backseat, slung a recyclable tote bag over my shoulder, and made my way inside.

# Chapter Five

# Ryan

"This isn't healthy. Not at all."

I turned to find Willa watching me from the corner as I followed the new blonde tenant around the apartment. She was unpacking her things, which was fascinating to me. Most of her belongings seemed handmade, but not in a cheesy, macaroni jewelry sort of way. Everything was unique, expertly crafted by hands that knew what they were doing.

"Healthy is a moot point," I shot back. "Don't you think?"

"It's creepy, Ryan. Stop that! Stop staring at her stuff." She shooed me out of the kitchen and into the living room.

"Well, Willa, there are only so many hours I can spend staring out the window and according to you I can't leave the apartment so what else am I supposed to do?"

"Gee, I don't know," she said, crossing her arms. "Maybe you could sit your butt down, close your eyes, and contemplate the life you just finished living."

"And what good would that do me? I'm dead. I can't change anything."

"No, but contemplation might give you some insight as to why you ended up here. With me. And it might also help you figure out how to move on, how to cross over."

"Doubtful."

Willa shook her head, disappointed when I went back to peeking in boxes and watching my guest unpack. "You're never getting out of here. Not at this rate."

The way she said those words, with a sense of deliberate suggestion, was not lost on me. My eyes snapped up to meet hers. "You know why I'm here. Don't you?"

She nodded.

"Then why don't you just tell me? Tell me what I did to deserve being imprisoned in this dump and then tell me what in the hell I have to do to get out of here. Don't just stand around all day scolding me for doing the only interesting thing I *can* do."

"Her name is Mercy."

"What?"

Willa nodded her head toward the blonde who had begun unpacking a box of books and I tilted my head to read the spines. Most of them were well worn, like she'd read them time and time again, but I didn't recognize any of the titles so I turned back to Willa.

She was gone.

"Thank God," I grumbled.

Glad to finally be rid of my babysitter, I turned back to the girl. Mercy? I'd always associated those five letters with benevolence or compassion, but had never run across anyone who wore it as their identity. It was a beautiful name.

Beautiful name for a beautiful woman.

"Mercy..."

She froze.

I froze.

Neither of us breathed as we waited for something to happen. Well, she didn't breathe. I just... went on not breathing. Had she heard me? Surely not. I moved closer and sure enough, the hair at the nape of her neck was standing on end, accompanied by a wave of goosebumps.

"You can hear me. Can't you?"

Mercy whirled around. Her wide eyes flew from one side of the room to the other, looking right through me.

"Who- who's there? Hello?"

I moved closer to her ear, ready to answer, exhilarated that she could hear me.

"Bad idea."

I stumbled back, caught off guard by Willa's voice. Shooting a look over my shoulder, I found her sitting on the arm of the couch, dangling her legs off the side as she braided her hair into pig tails.

"Why is it a bad idea?"

Willa cocked her head to the side. "Do you really want the list?"

"Uh, yeah, actually I do."

"Fine. Reason one: You're dead. You're supposed to be silent."

"Yeah, well she's not *supposed* to be able to hear me either," I shot back.

"Exactly. And two wrongs don't make a right. Nothing good can come of this. So, why don't you just sit down and shut your trap."

"I thought angels were supposed to be nice. You're kind of a pain in the-"

"Hey! Watch yourself," she warned. "I'm not an angel."

"I'll say." I laughed as I watched Mercy out of the corner of my eye. She was still shaken, but doing her best to ignore what she'd heard. "So, if you're not an angel, then what are..."

I blinked and Willa was gone. Again.

"You seriously need to stop doing that."

# Mercy

By the time Monday rolled around, I was more than ready to be out of my apartment for the day. Aside from feeling like I was being watched, I was starting to hear voices. One time, I could have sworn someone had said my name. And like an idiot, I'd responded.

Even if there was some kind of spirit energy residing in my apartment, I knew better than to try and reach out. That always ended in disaster. My mother and father would have told me to cleanse the place or attempt to help the spirit cross over, but I didn't plan on doing either of those things. I was going to do what any other normal person would do in my situation. I was going to ignore it until it went away.

My first day at my new job was nothing like I expected it to be. Everyone in the office was rude, conniving, grumpy, and seemed overall dissatisfied with their lot in life. The idea that my parents had been right about working in the corporate world kept sneaking into my head, but I repeatedly told that idea to shove it.

They couldn't be right. I wouldn't let them. Everyone else might hate their job, but that didn't mean I had to. I was determined to enjoy the monotony, make a few friends, and make enough money to live comfortably on my own.

"Ready to take lunch?" Drew asked at a quarter til noon.

"Absolutely."

I was starving. For some insane reason, I'd put off grocery shopping and all I'd had to eat before going into work was a leftover bowl of wonton soup from the night before. And it wasn't filling. At all.

Drew and I headed down to the break room, nodding at everyone we passed in silent acknowledgment but not sparing the time or energy to smile or say hello. I'd used the last of the food I brought with me from Indiana to make a sack lunch consisting of a peanut butter and apple jelly sandwich on peta bread, a banana, and a kale salad. At first I feared that my homemade lunch would look juvenile in a place as sophisticated as the building we worked in, but that thought was quickly put to rest when I spied Drew's lunch. Three Lunchables in a plastic bag.

The break room was still mostly empty since most people didn't take their breaks until after noon. It was only us and two women I recognized from the filing room. A redhead who kept her nose in the air at all times and a brunette with beautiful blue eyes and some of the longest eyelashes I'd ever seen on a human being. Drew later informed me that they were fake. Which made me laugh.

"I want a thigh gap so freaking bad," the

brunette said as she poured a cup of coffee.

"I know, right? Thigh gaps are so hot right now."

Drew approached the women and I followed, not knowing what else to do. They both grew quiet as Drew poured himself a cup of coffee and began loading it with cream and sugar. I looked up to find the brunette staring at me like I'd just killed her cat.

"Hi, I'm Mercy. I'm new." I extended my hand.

The redhead snorted. "Mercy? That's your name? Seriously?"

"Uh, yeah?"

"Don't pay them any mind." Drew took my arm and steered me toward a table in the corner.

"Don't you think so, Drew?" The brunette questioned, totally ignoring the fact that we were trying to leave.

"Don't I think what?"

"Thigh gaps," she said, batting her eyelashes. "Sexy, right?"

Drew scoffed as we continued walking away. "Not my thing," he called back. "But don't worry. You have a pretty impressive brain gap, and that's so much sexier."

I bit my lip to keep from laughing as the two women cursed beneath their breath and clicked out of the room on their shiny, patent leather heels.

*So much for making friends.*


Pushing a mail cart through busy hallways and weaving around cubicles was one heck of a workout. By the time I arrived home, all I wanted to do was crash. I finished unpacking the night before and didn't have laundry or dishes to do so I flopped down on the couch and grabbed a magazine out of my purse that had been discarded in the mail room.

Flipping through the glossy pages, I expected to find at least one article that could hold my attention. Instead, all I encountered were ads for different brands of makeup, workout routines, and low-carb recipes. None of it even remotely interested me, but I made an effort to read a portion of the articles, knowing that *this* was what women in the city -normal women- fawned over and spent their days discussing.

As I was thinking back and wondering why the women in the break room had been so obsessed over a couple of empty inches between their thighs, the apartment grew quiet. Eerily so.

Every day since I had moved in, I'd been greeted by the sudden stillness and every time it happened, it doubled in intensity. I was growing accustomed to it, but it still made my heart beat a little louder and my breathing turn erratic.

Brushing it off, I focused on the page I was attempting to read in an effort to ignore whatever was going on in the room. But as I continued to read, the hairs on the back of my neck stood on end and goosebumps erupted along my fair skin. *That* I couldn't ignore. I sat up and dropped the magazine to the table before looked around the room.

Nothing.

"I'm going crazy." I laughed to myself as I fished my phone out of my pocket, desperate for a distraction.

Drew had insisted that I needed a Facebook,

Twitter, and Instagram account to be a fully functioning adult and I wasn't sure why, but scrolling through my feeds made me chuckle. Mostly, I was friends with people Drew suggested, and they seemed to be a lively bunch. They posted pictures of everything from their morning coffee mugs, to their after-work cocktails. From their freshly applied morning makeup, to their meals neatly arranged on fine China. Why they thought these things were important enough to share with the world was beyond me.

Movement in my peripheral vision caught my attention and my eyes darted up from the phone.

Screaming, I launched myself off the couch and pressed my back against the wall. There, in my kitchen, was a strange man leaning against the counter, silently staring at me.

"Wha-what do you want?" I shrieked.

I grabbed for my purse and dug through looking for the bottle of pepper spray Drew had insisted I buy on my first night in the city. Once my shaky hands wrapped around the small plastic container, I lifted it like a gun and aimed it at the intruder after tossing my purse to the floor.

"Get out! Get out now!"

The man in the kitchen looked confused as he darted his eyes around the apartment.

"I'm serious. Get out or I'm calling the cops!"

He turned his blue eyes over his shoulder, focused back on me, then shook his head in disbelief.

"You can see me?"

"Of course I can see you, idiot! You're standing in the middle of my kitchen! Now get out!"

"Oh my God!" He yelled. "Oh my God, you can see me!"

Then he ran to me.

Screaming, I turned my face and pressed the button on the pepper spray as a mixture of fear and adrenaline dumped into my system. I waited for the groans of discomfort from the man I'd just sprayed, but the room was quiet. There were no agonized screams like I expected, but my arms were shaking so badly I found it hard to stay upright.

Tears gathered in my eyes as I fought against the hormone that sent my heart to racing. I was the opposite of an adrenaline junkie. I hated the high. Unlike other people, it made me unfocused, dizzy, and breathless.

My mouth went dry and I tried to swallow around the lump in my throat. I knew I had to open my eyes but I was too busy being a coward. Shaking my head, hoping it was all just a bad dream, I cracked my eyes.

Everything was a blur.

A really freaking painful blur.

I dropped the bottle to the floor and covered my eyes as they filled with tears. "Oh my God, that burns! What the hell?! Oh my God, oh my God, oh my God!"

"Well, it's pepper spray, of course it burns. That's kinda the point."

I cringed away from the voice, unable to open my eyes.

"What do you want? I don't have anything valuable, I swear." My voice broke as I failed to hold myself together. If he wanted money, he was out of

70

luck. If he wanted to rob me, well, he was going to be disappointed.

"Are you okay? You really need to flush your eyes out with water." His voice followed me as I tried to get away.

"What do you want!?" I screamed again. "Why are you in my apartment?"

"You really need to get to the bathroom. It's just going to get worse the longer you keep your eyes closed," he said. His voice was even and deep, serious but with a trace of humor beneath the surface. "Using pepper spray in such a small room isn't exactly the best of ideas, you know."

His voice didn't sound threatening, but that still didn't negate the fact that he was in my home, where he wasn't welcome.

"Yeah, I got that. Now can you please get the hell out!" I parted my eyes enough to see him reach for me. "Don't touch me!"

He drew back before crossing his arms and turning to look across the room. "Couldn't even if I wanted to," he muttered before nodding his head in my direction. "How can she see me?"

I followed his eyes, painfully, since my eyelids were starting to swell, but there was no one else in the room. It was just us.

"Who... who are you talking to?"

His brown eyebrows furrowed as he looked back and forth between me and my dresser, me and my dresser, me and my dresser.

"Uh, no one," he said uncertainly. "Look, you really do need you rinse your eyes out."

He moved closer and instead of cringing away,

I lashed out. With my fist aimed at his chest, I swung for all I was worth.

And punched the wall.

"Gah!" I held my throbbing hand to my chest. "What the-?"

I looked up at the stranger, who was looking down at me with one quirked eyebrow, completely unruffled by the fact that I'd just attacked him. He had to be crazy. Crazy, and maybe dangerous.

Gathering up my courage, as well as pocketing my pacifistic instincts, I pulled my leg back and moved to kick his shin as hard as I could.

And I watched as my foot sailed through his leg and met no resistance.

"Would you stop? You're going to hurt yourself."

"Oh my God," I whispered before meeting his eyes. "I'm losing my mind. You're not even here, are you? You're just... you're just a figment of my imagination. Or- or maybe that magazine was laced with something. Yeah. I'm on an acid trip, aren't I?" I laughed as I made my way to my feet. I was either seeing things, or I was going crazy. Or both.

I pressed myself back against the wall, shaky and disoriented from the adrenaline. Or from my psychotic break, I wasn't sure. Reaching out, I grabbed for his arm... and felt nothing.

Again, I reached to touch him. My hand met empty, frigid air with every swipe.

I covered my mouth to keep from laughing. "Oh, thank goodness, you're not real."

"Eh, about as real as a shadow. Real as pain or love or happiness." He looked across the room and shrugged.

"Riiiight." I began to circle him like a buzzard, amazed by how much detail my brain could throw into one hallucination.

He watched, quietly entertained, as I continued to wave my hand through his body.

"You're a little out there, aren't ya?"

"What?" I met his eyes, and just for good measure tried to run my fingers through his light brown hair. I couldn't. He wasn't there. He wasn't real.

"Uh, can we start over without me terrifying you or you trying to molest my head?" He reached his hand out in greeting, but then grimaced and dropped it to his side. "I'm Ryan. Ryan Callahan."

And that's when my eyes rolled to the back of my skull and I hit the floor.

# Chapter Six

## Ryan

"Well, that went well," Willa laughed. "Don't you think?"

"Shut up! What do I do?"

"Kudos on the attempted rescue, by the way. Nice dive."

"She was falling. It was instinct. Stop laughing!"

Willa waved her arms around, mimicking my actions. "Her face just went white and you were all, 'Oh, no!'" She roared out in laughter again. "And then THUNK! Out cold!"

"Could you stop, please? You are the least helpful person on the planet, you know that?"

"Hey pal!" In a second, the teasing light left her voice, only to be replaced by a severe edge that had me looking up to find her tiny finger pointed at my face. "I warned you not to do it, but you didn't listen. So this," she pointed to Mercy resting on the floor, "is *your* fault."

Hanging my head, I sighed in defeat. She was right. If I'd just stayed away and kept my mouth shut, Mercy wouldn't be unconscious on the floor. But I couldn't bring myself to regret it. It felt so good to have someone see me, really *see* me. I don't know how it happened, and I didn't care. I just hoped it would happen again.

Taking a seat next to Mercy's resting body, I crossed my legs and propped my head on my closed fists. "Now what?"

"Well, you can't *undo* your brilliant little stunt, so now I guess you wait for her to wake up. Not much else you can do, lover boy."

I cut my eyes to her face. "Very funny."

"Ryan," Willa said slowly, fiddling with the ends of her hair, "What do you think you are?"

"A dead dude."

"Right, but aside from that."

"I don't know... a ghost? A spirit? A soul with unfinished business? Am I getting warmer?"

"Sort of." She came to sit beside me, careful to keep our bodies from touching. "You're a ghost, yes, but people don't come back as spirits for no reason and it's not something that happens every day. People aren't sent back because they're being punished either. A person's return *always* serves a purpose. So, I think you're here for a very specific, very important reason and I think it has something to do with that girl right there."

"You *think*? I thought you knew why I was

75

here, why I haven't moved on."

"I only know the end game."

"Which is?"

She cocked her head to the side, letting me know she wasn't about to divulge her secrets.

Frustrated, I buried my fingers in my hair, tugging on the ends. It was a weird sensation, not being able to actually feel the discomfort that would have grounded me when I was alive.

"So, I'm here for a reason, but you can't tell me what it is, because you don't even know. All you know is that I can't leave and I'm here because of her." I nodded at Mercy "And somehow, through lurking around the apartment and creeping her out, I'm supposed to come to some grand revelation about my life and death and figure out what part I'm supposed to play in the grand scheme of things. Is that what you're saying?"

She smiled, showcasing her tiny, pearly white teeth. "Glad we're on the same page."

"What page?" I asked incredulously. "None of that means anything to me."

"Not yet," she said, pointing at me. "But it will. One day."

"And until then?"

"Until then, you try not to let *this* happen again."

She gestured to Mercy and I buried my face in my hands. I'd never actually seen anyone faint before and I felt like a jerk for not being able to catch her, but that's yet another drawback to being dead.

"I think you're supposed to help her, Ryan."

"Help her? Help her do what?"

"I'm not sure. It's just a hunch," she shrugged. "And to address the other issue, I think Mercy could see you because you wanted her to. You wanted to be seen."

She was right. I had wanted to be seen, more than anything. I wanted to be seen and acknowledged and heard. And I'd gotten my wish, right before Mercy blacked out.

"Well, what about you?" I asked. "You don't want to be seen?"

"No, but I couldn't be seen even if I wanted to."

"Why?"

Did I possess some kind of power she didn't? Or did she just abide by whatever cosmic rule it was that I wasn't privy to?

Willa smiled that same knowing smile I'd grown so familiar with. "Because, Ryan, I'm not a ghost."

Mercy groaned and I cocked my head to see if she was coming to. She didn't seem to be.

"Then what are you?"

My eyes had only moved for a split second, but Willa was gone. Again.

"I really hate it when you do that."

# Mercy

I awoke to a low voice whispering next to me. My eyes were sore, swollen, and felt like they were being assaulted by the fires of hell every time I tried to open them. So even though I wanted to open my eyes and locate the hushed voice, I couldn't.

"Who's there?" My voice sounded like gravel against a cheese grater.

"Me. Ryan," the voice answered.

"Ugh, so it wasn't a dream." I felt around without opening my eyes and found the edge of the couch and used it to pull myself up. "I would tell you to get out, but apparently you don't listen well."

"No, I don't. But I'm not a threat, I promise. Couldn't hurt you even if I tried."

"Oh yes, the fact that I can barely see and I have a huge knot on my head is testament to that fact."

"Hey, that was all your doing." His voice sounded closer, and I jerked my head away from the noise.

"Is someone else here? Who were you talking to?"

He let out an aggravated snort. "I don't know, God?"

"God? You... you're talking to God?"

"I don't know. And if I was, I wouldn't so much be talking to him as I would be questioning his motives."

"That doesn't sound like the smartest thing to do," I replied.

"It's not."

I managed to open my left eye and look around the room. Ryan was sitting Indian-style on the floor. "Uh huh, well, as awkwardly terrifying as this little meet-n-greet has been, I think you should leave now." I pulled my shoulders back and looked away, trying to make it clear that he was not welcome.

"Trust me," he said, his voice laced with annoyance, "I'd love to."

"Well, there's the door." I pointed in the general direction of the exit.

"Yes. I can see that, thank you," he deadpanned, making me feel like a moron for pointing it out.

"Well, go. Or walk through the wall or float away, or do whatever it is you do."

"It's not that simple."

Ryan stood and crossed his arms, looking down at me as if *I* were the one keeping him from leaving.

I wasn't.

He took one step across the room and stopped when his legs rested within the coffee table like it wasn't even there. Looking up, watching him as he towered over me, I felt small, insignificant, and completely overwhelmed by the very idea of his existence.

"Maybe it's the phone," I blurted.

He tilted his head as if he hadn't heard me. "What?"

"My cell phone. Maybe my parents were right. Maybe it's frying my brain."

Ryan's blue eyes glittered with laughter but he didn't say a word, didn't crack a smile. Instead, he just shook his head.

"Or maybe it's the burger I ate yesterday. Maybe the steroids or chemicals or whatever they put in it are messing with my head. Yeah, that has to be it. OR!" I yelled, "Maybe someone slipped magic mushrooms into my lunch."

Ryan shook his head slowly. "Because all those things sound so much more reasonable than a ghost living in your apartment?"

I shot him a look as I tried to keep a straight face. "A ghost *living* in my apartment?"

"Whatever." He moved across the room to look out the window. "Residing, haunting, dwelling, inhabiting, occupying. Take your pick."

"Okay, Mr. Thesaurus, what if I don't believe in ghosts?"

It was a theoretical question. I did believe in ghosts. Very much so.

He shrugged. "Believe in me or not, doesn't make a difference. I'm still here."

True. But I knew there had to be ways to make him leave and I didn't plan on coming home to a tortured soul everyday.

"What if I ignore you? Will you disappear?"

He scoffed, but didn't look back to meet my eyes. So, I turned away and focused all my energy on the room, my body, the sounds outside... anything but the man staring out the window. I meditated on every living thing around me, hoping to banish all the non-living things.

"I don't know why you're trying so hard to get rid of me. I was here first."

My still tear-filled eyes snapped open and I spun around. "Because I'm not Demi Moore!" I yelled. "This isn't Ghost and you shouldn't be here!"

He shook his head, but still didn't face me. "I hated that movie."

"Of course you did. You're a guy."

"That pottery scene was pretty hot though, right?" He finally turned to face me and I felt my cheeks heat as he winked and the corner of his mouth lifted up in a half-smile.

"I'm ignoring you."

He sighed and went back to creeping on the people milling around on the sidewalk below. "Suit yourself."

Slumping down onto the couch, I was determined to act as if he didn't exist and I was completely alone. I grabbed the magazine off the table and flipped through it, hoping I looked nonchalant and completely aloof. But the burning behind my eyelids kept the pages from coming into focus. Even though I didn't spray myself directly, the particles in the mist had still made their way into my eyes.

I blinked repeatedly, hoping my tears would

flush out the sting so I wouldn't have to get up, but the burn intensified. After a few minutes, I couldn't see anything.

"Do you plan on flushing your eyes out? Or do you enjoy slowly going blind?"

I bounced my foot and proceeded to act like I was reading the magazine. In reality, I was dying a slow death from my eyeballs out, but I wasn't one to crack under pressure. I wasn't going to acknowledge his presence, let alone his suggestion. Even though that suggestion sounded really, really good with each passing second.

"Whatever," he said. "Eyes are overrated, right? The whole seeing thing, it's so mainstream. Way to be a rebel."

He was mocking me, laughing without actually laughing. But I wouldn't cave. I wouldn't let him win. Whether he was a ghost or just a figment of my imagination, I didn't plan on letting him having any kind of effect on me.

Until my throat began to close.

Coughing and sputtering, I threw the magazine to the floor and beat on my chest. Like that would help. There was a five-alarm fire burning it's way through my esophagus.

"Water, Mercy. For the love of God, go get a freaking drink and rinse your eyes out."

Fighting for breathe, I refused to move from the couch. I wouldn't give him the satisfaction. Why? Because I'm a stubborn idiot.

"You'd really rather writhe in pain than listen to me. Seriously?"

*Yes. Seriously.*

82

I grabbed a tissue off the side table and blew my nose, which too was starting to burn.

"This is ridiculous," I heard my uninvited guess say in exasperation. "Look at me."

I shook my head vigorously, sending tears scattering across the couch.

"Mercy!"

His commanding tone caught me off guard and I lifted my head to find him crouched on the floor in front of me. Before I knew what he was planning to do, he leaned forward and blew in my face.

I jerked back in surprise, but instantly calmed when a gust of cool, soothing air caressed my eyes and started to eased the burn. Slowly, the fire in my ocular cavity dulled and the tears ceased long enough for me to blink through the haze. I could see.

"Better?"

I wasn't about to admit that he had helped me, and really, I didn't even understand how. Dead people don't heal the living. That's a fact.

"I'm going to bed," I croaked before standing and stomping to the bathroom, ready to put the entire day behind me. Hopefully, when I woke the next day, I'd come to realize this was all just a silly dream.

"You're welcome," Ryan whispered sarcastically as I closed the door behind me. And because I apparently couldn't do anything right or anything that made a lick of sense, I locked the door behind me.

# Chapter Seven

# Ryan

      While Mercy slept, I sat quietly and listened to the clinking of dishes coming from The Mayflower, the Chinese restaurant down the street. In life, I'd always loved the way Chinatown never seemed to sleep or the way everything always smelled like fried food. Always. It seeped into people's clothing, into their hair, and left a permanent stain to the air. It was so persistent that when I first moved there, I had spent countless nights dreaming that I was being chased by egg rolls dressed as samurais.

      I laughed, recalling the ridiculous dream, but my laughter quickly died away as I realized I'd never again dream. Dreaming was meant for the living. When you're dead, you have nothing left to dream for. I was incapable of dreaming. I no longer had firing synapses, no conscious and subconscious, no ambition, no emotions. No future. My past was all anyone would ever know about me. And what an unimpressive past that had been.

"Don't you have anything better to do?"

I tilted my head back to find Willa perched on the arm of the couch. The legs of her pink overalls were rolled up to the knee like she'd been playing in a creek. Her bare feet dangled in the air as she smiled and gestured to me sulking at the window, which had become my favorite past time.

"No, not really."

"Are you sure?" She tilted her head to the side and pursed her lips.

"Well, what would you suggest? Other than 'try to figure out why you're here', because that hasn't been working out to well for me."

One of Willa's tiny shoulders lifted in a half-shrug as she hopped up and started walking across the back of the couch like it was a balance beam. "You could find a way to be useful."

"Useful. Me?" I said sarcastically. "What possible use could I be to anyone?"

Willa stopped in her tracks and dropped to the floor before tilting her head to the side and raising a hand to me. "Do you hear something?"

"What? No, I-"

I clamped my jaw shut.

There was something. It was quiet, but it was there. I looked around, focusing on the noise. After pinpointing the disturbance, I walked to the door and glanced out the peephole.

"Who is that?"

Willa never answered, and I didn't bother

turning around. I knew she was gone.

Pressing my hands to the door, I peered out into the deserted hallway where a man clad in black was down on his knees, attempting to pick the lock. I knew how easily the apartment doors could be breached. Home invasions weren't common in the apartments, especially since Alice kept the doors to the lobby closed after hours, but they still happened. In the year I'd lived there, there had been three on my floor.

The lock began to turn, getting closer to being cracked with every click.

I had to wake Mercy.

Sprinting to the bedroom, I found her curled in a ball, sleeping soundly. Too soundly.

"Mercy, wake up!"

She didn't stir.

"Mercy! Mercy!" I reached out and smoothed my hand across her face, which did nothing. I couldn't feel her, but I hoped that she could feel me, feel the cool air of my presence.

"Mercy, please, you have to get up. Now!"

I stopped cold when a beam of light sliced across the room, cutting through the darkness and landing at my feet.

He was inside.

"Mercy!" I screamed her name, but it was no use.

She couldn't hear me and I couldn't shake her awake. I also couldn't do anything about the man creeping through her kitchen.

Cursing beneath my breath, I shook my hands out nervously as I looked around the room, feeling more helpless than when I watched Mercy faint and slip through my fingers. But with a burglar, or whatever he was, inside the apartment, there was more at stake than just a bump on the head. Mercy could get seriously hurt. Or worse.

Panicking, I searched the room for a sign, for anything that could possibly help me. But I couldn't be heard, couldn't touch, couldn't do something as simple as lift Mercy's cell phone off the table.

Glancing at that little piece of technology, I remembered my sister's phone call, how the ringing was altered when I came in contact with the phone.

Hoping that I could manipulate other kinds of electronics, I sprung toward the small radio sitting on the dresser. Mercy had turned the volume down low enough you couldn't make out the words, but loud enough it served as white noise to help her sleep.

"God, I hope this works."

Bracing my hands on either side of the speakers, I closed my eyes and focused all my energy, all my being, on one word: *Loud.*

Instantly, as if in answer to my prayer, the volume skyrocketed and I turned to find Mercy bolting up in bed the same time the masked intruder tripped over the coffee table in his haste to escape.

"Ryan?"

Mercy's eyes shot wide as her head swung back and forth in confusion.

"Look!" I yelled, not knowing what else to say.

Mercy glanced around the corner and without a second thought, jumped for the wall and flipped on the light, bathing the intruder in a blinding, yellow glow.

Mercy and I watched as the robber tripped over his own feet as he tried to right himself. Judging by Mercy's labored breathing, she was scared speechless, but thankfully, she was awake. Which, after thinking about it, presented a whole new problem.

If he just wanted to steal from her, he could have done that and then left her in peace. But if he wanted something else, she was in danger, and absolutely nothing I could do would help her. All I had was my voice and the only person I could communicate with was Mercy.

Remembering her reaction to me, I realized that was enough.

"Mercy!" I yelled. "Pepper spray!"

Without missing a beat, she snatched her purse off the nightstand, upended it on the bed, grabbed the tiny bottle, and took aim.

"Get out!" Her voice rang out clear and confident as she stood, legs shoulder width apart, hands out in front of her, and chin pulled up in a strong show of self-assurance.

It wasn't a gun, but that didn't seem to matter. The man didn't have to be told twice. As soon as he managed to get his feet beneath him, he took off running for the door. To my astonishment, Mercy followed him, not showing even an ounce of fear as she watched him flee down the hall before shutting and locking the door behind him.

"Wow."

Mercy braced her hand against the door and closed her eyes before taking a deep, stuttering breath.

When she opened her eyes again, she turned to face me. Only then could I see the fear cracking through her tough exterior. She wasn't fearless, of course she wasn't. Her move to advance on the man had been straight out of the first chapter of Self-preservation 101.

"That was... impressive," I said as she crossed the room and quieted the radio.

She stood with her back to me, both arms braced against the front of the dresser with her chin resting on her chest. I fought the urge to go to her, to place my hand on her shoulder and tell her how amazing that show of strength had been.

"I should call Mrs. Whitlock."

"And maybe the cops," I suggested.

Mercy picked up her cell phone and dialed Alice's number, but just as she pressed the phone to her ear, there was a knock at the door.

"Mercy, dear? Are you awake?" Mrs. Whitlock called softly.

"What is she doing here? It's one in the morning. She shouldn't be out of bed."

I followed Mercy to the door. "And yet you were just about to wake her with a phone call."

She opened the door and we both stood in the threshold, surprised to Mrs. Whitlock shaking and holding a cordless phone to her chest.

"Are you alright?" She asked as she reached out for Mercy's hand.

"Yes, I'm fine. But how'd you know that-"

"Dave from across the hall," she interrupted. "He's a very light sleeper and heard the commotion. Called and said he saw someone leave your apartment all in a tizzy. But don't you worry dear, I've called the police and they're on their way."

"Oh, Mrs. Whitlock, you really didn't have to do that. It could have waited til morning."

"Nonsense! You could have been hurt!"

"But I'm fine, really. He didn't even take anything." She moved out of the way so Alice could see inside. "See. Just scuffed up my coffee table. I woke up when Ry- I mean... when I heard him making noise and I turned on the lights and grabbed my pepper spray. Sent him running."

The nonchalance in her voice sent a wave of admiration through my chest. She wasn't just trying to act brave because she wanted people to know she was okay on her own; she was brushing it off so Alice wouldn't worry.

"Oh, you brave girl," Alice said. "I would have screamed the place down."

"Knock knock."

We all turned to find a young policeman standing in the open door.

"Oh, Neil! There you are." Alice grabbed the cop by the arm and practically dragged him into the living room. "This here's Mercy Hunter. She was almost robbed, but get this! She grabbed that little can of pepper spray right there and he took off running for the hills. Bet you don't see *that* everyday!"

Neil's eyes took their time running from Mercy's messy hair all the way down to her bare feet, taking in every little detail along the way. And my hackles rose.

"No," he said. "I definitely don't see that everyday." He extended his hand to Mercy. "Officer

Whitlock."

"Mercy Hunter." She shook his hand and offered him a pleasant smile.

"What a schmuck," I said, earning me a death glare. "Seriously, did you not just see the way he sized you up? Ten bucks says he's guessing your bra size right now."

"Hush," she whispered.

Neil cocked his head to the side as he placed both hands in his pockets. "Excuse me?"

"What?" Mercy looked up, wide eyed and embarrassed to be caught talking to 'herself'. "Sorry, I-uh... guess I'm still not totally awake."

"Or you're in shock. Common with things like this," Neil supplied as he took out a tiny pad of paper and a pen. "Now, is there anything you can tell me about this guy? Height, weight, hair color, ethnicity? Anything like that?"

"Well, I didn't really get a good look at him."

"Oh for Pete's sake," I said, stepping in between Mercy and Neil. "He was about five foot ten, maybe weighed around two fifteen, and had dark eyes."

Mercy was trying her hardest to avoid looking me in the eyes, but she was at least listening.

"Actually, now that I have a second to think about it, I think maybe it was a little taller than me. Five ten, maybe? And if I had to guess, probably two hundred and fifteen-ish pounds. And um, I couldn't really see his face through the mask, but I think he had dark eyes."

Neil scribbled as she talked, glancing up every line or two to cast Mercy the most shameless set of

91

'come hither' eyes I'd ever seen on a man.

"That's all I can really tell you," Mercy said apologetically. "He just broke in, I woke up, flipped the lights on, grabbed my pepper spray, and told him to get out. And then he left. That's it."

"Okay," Neil nodded. "Well, we'll definitely look into it."

"Pssht, yeah right," I mumbled.

Mercy cleared her throat, obviously trying to tell me to shut my trap in that subtle way of hers.

"Well, thank you, Officer..." Mercy squinted her eyes to read his tiny name plate. "Whitlock?"

Alice put her arms around Neil's waist and pulled him in for an awkward hug. "That's right. My favorite grandson."

"Her only grandson," he said, carefully extracting himself from his grandmother's python grip.

"Oh, give her your card, Neil," Alice said excitedly. "Just in case she remembers anything."

Neil sighed and I couldn't help but laugh at the way his grandmother was making him seem like a rent-a-cop fresh on the job.

"Here you go, ma'am. That's my work number right there, the station number below that, and my personal line is on the back."

"Oooh, personal line." I rolled my eyes. He was too much.

However, Alice didn't seem to think so. Her bright blue eyes bounced between Mercy and her beloved grandson, already picturing their future children, no doubt.

"He's a little old for you, don't you think?" The

92

words fell from my mouth without ever passing through my brain-to-mouth filter. "I mean... guy's gotta be in his mid to late twenties, right?"

"Alright," Mercy said loudly. "Well, thanks for stopping by! If I think of anything else I'll be sure to give you a call. And thanks for everything, Mrs. Whitlock. You really didn't have to go through all this trouble."

"Oh, of course I did!" Alice looked back as Mercy steered her and her grandson to the door. "I want to make sure you're safe and taken care of here. No burglar is going to get away with robbing one of my tenants, no siree."

"Well, thanks again. Nice meeting you, Neil."

Mercy waved politely but before Officer Meat Head could reply, she shut and locked the door. Breathing out a sigh of relief, she turned on me and narrowed her striking blue eyes.

"That was a little much, don't you think?"

"I'm sorry. What?"

There could have been a million things she was referring to, and I wasn't sure which way her emotional pendulum would swing, so I waited for her to explain.

"Were you just sitting in the chair watching me sleep? Or standing over me listening to me breathe? Do you honest to God not have anything better to do?" She crossed her arms and marched back to her room.

Naturally, I followed.

"Don't make me out to be some slimy pervert, okay. And frankly, I'm insulted by your insinuation. I was just looking out the window, minding my own business when Joe-Bob-whatever-his-name-is starting jimmying your lock."

"Uh huh," she replied, clearly unconvinced.

I didn't know what to say. I'd just done her a colossal favor and instead of being grateful, she somehow managed to spin the entire situation around to make *me* seem like the bad guy.

Mercy stopped by the edge of the bed and turned to face me. Her mouth was set in a defiant line, but her eyes glistened with unshed tears, telling me that she was nearing her breaking point.

"Please, Ryan." Her voice shook and my eyes dropped down to her trembling bottom lip. "I need you to leave. Please. This is just... it's to much."

Running my hands through my hair, I turned away from her and stared at the door. I couldn't leave. Willa had made that perfectly clear- as had all the times I'd tried to 'ghost' my way through the walls. No matter how much Mercy wanted to be alone -and I understood that need completely- I couldn't grant her that.

I also couldn't figure out how to turn off whatever had been flipped on when she first caught sight of me. So, I did the closest thing to leaving that I could manage. I moved into the living room and turned my back on her. Ignoring her probably wouldn't give her any solace whatsoever, but it was all I could do.

"That's not leaving," she said, "that's about the equivalent of a child covering their eyes so the world won't see them."

"Well sorry, but I can't just walk through the door."

"Can't or won't?" She shot back.

I'd had enough.

"Can't, Mercy! I can't leave!" I exploded. "I've tried. Don't you think I've tried to leave a thousand freaking times? It. Doesn't. Work. It wasn't my idea to burden you with my presence so you're just going to have to put up with me until I figure out how to get the hell out of here. You're not the one trapped here. I am. You're not the one who died. I am. You're not the one who has no freaking clue what's going on. So, I'm sorry if I'm such an inconvenience, but there's not a damn thing I can do about it."

Mercy didn't fire back. She just stood, immobile, as I fought to calm myself. I wasn't the kind of man who lashed out at women, especially those I barely knew, but I was at the end of my rope. I didn't mean to snap, but it was done. As soon as I finished yelling, I immediately wished I could take the words back. Just grab 'em out of thin air and shove 'em back down my throat.

"I'm sorry," she breathed after a minute. "I didn't mean to-"

"I shouldn't have yelled," I blurted. "And for that, I'm sorry. But I saved your life, Mercy. Okay, maybe that's taking it a little far, but I *helped* you! And this is the thanks I get? Seriously?" I turned to face her. "You're being ridiculous."

Mercy's entire shell broke as her lips cracked into a smile, catching me completely off guard. What was it with this woman? I had been ready to throw my hands up to protect my face from her laser vision, but her death glare was gone. Vanished. In it's place, was a coy, playful smile.

"I'm being ridiculous?" She covered her mouth to silence a giggle. "I'm in my pajamas, standing in the middle of my apartment, talking to a dead guy at two o'clock in the morning. If that's not ridiculous..."

She trailed off, but I understood.

"Look, I'm sorry if me being here freaks you out, but I wasn't trying to be a creep. Scout's honor." I held up two fingers and placed a hand over my heart.

Mercy rolled her eyes. "Scout's honor is three fingers."

I dropped my arms to my sides. "Whatever. I was never a boy scout."

"Right." Mercy's smile faded as she dropped her eyes to the floor. "Look, I'm sorry. I shouldn't have called you a creep. That was cruel of me. Besides, you *were* here first. Who am I to question why you haven't left?"

That wasn't the kind of response I'd been anticipating, but I was thankful nonetheless.

"Thank you." Her smile returned at the sincerity in my voice. "If I could change things, I would, but I can't. So, thank you for respecting that."

"You're welcome."

Not knowing what else to say, I glanced at the clock on the wall and realized Mercy had only had a couple hours of sleep.

*Way to keep Creeper Tabs on her...*

"Well, you should probably get back to bed. You've got work tomorrow, right?"

"Right," she nodded.

I stepped across the room and reclaimed my usual spot at the window. I'm not sure what I was looking for day after day, but something about

96

watching the street made me feel *right*. Like it was my station; my post to stand watch.

With my back to the room, I listened as Mercy flipped the light and crawled back into bed. I had absolutely no idea how she planned to sleep after what just happened, but she needed her rest if she was still planning on going to work in a few hours.

Anyone else would have tossed and turned for hours, I know I would have, but not Mercy. I kept one ear trained on her as she began a series of breathing exercises that reminded me of a cross between yoga breathing and lamaze. I listened to each inhale. Each exhale. I tried to picture, tried to remember what it was like to breathe. What it was like to not feel submerged in water, pulling your heavy limbs behind you as you tried to drag yourself across the bottom of a never-ending ocean.

After roughly fifty breaths, she hummed in complacency and made herself comfortable.

Even though I had zero adrenaline to my name, just listening to Mercy relaxed me. Maybe it was due to the fact that I knew she was safe. Maybe it was the cute humming noises she made as she snuggled into her pillow. Or maybe it was the rhythmic sound of her slowed breathing.

Whatever it was, I felt calm. At ease. Peaceful.

"Ryan?" She called out sleepily.

"Yeah?" I glanced over my shoulder and caught sight of her nestled in the center of the bed, surrounded by thick pillows and colorful blankets.

"Thank you."

I turned back around. I had to. With the moonlight filtering in through the blinds, casting a porcelain glow across her face, she was too beautiful to stand. Factor in the sincerity of her voice and, like an idiot, I was fighting a surge of happiness at being in the same room with such a creature.

"You're welcome, Mercy." Even I was struck by the way my voice caressed her name, so I quickly cleared my throat and focused my eyes back out across the darkened Chicago landscape. "Now, go back to sleep."

# Mercy

"You look like hell!" Drew exclaimed as he met me in the elevator bay.

"Thank you. That's exactly the kind of greeting I was hoping for."

"Sorry. Rough night?" He handed me a hot tea out of the drink carrier he was juggling, but whipped it out of my reach at the last second. "Or *fun* night?"

"Rough," I answered. "Very rough. Now, can I have my tea or are you going to make me stab you in the jugular with my pen?"

"Ouch. That bad?" Thankfully, Drew relented and handed me the steaming cup I'd been so looking forward to all morning.

"Yeah, that bad."

"And I'm guessing from your ice queen glare and piss-off posture you don't really wanna talk about it?"

"You're investigative skills are as keen as ever."

"They really are," he said as we stepped into

the elevator. "I really shouldn't be wasting all this potential working in a mail room. I could be off solving cases for the CIA or the FBI."

I laughed with him as we descended into the basement, surrounded by other worker from the mail room, all of which waved at or chatted with Drew briefly before the elevator dinged and we all exited the confined space.

"Got any plans after work?"

"After work?" I hitched my purse strap higher on my shoulder as we made our way down the hall. "I haven't even clocked in yet. I'm not thinking that far ahead. Why?"

"Thought you might wanna grab dinner at The Mayflower or something."

I didn't. I had more important things to do, like figure out why I had an undead tenant keeping tabs on me.

"Maybe some other time. I don't think I'd be very good company tonight."

"And why's that?"

I lifted and dropped my shoulder in a half-shrug. "Just got a lot on my mind right now."

"Anything I can help you with?" He smiled his trademark lopsided grin as we punched our time cards. Drew really was a good friend, and I was thankful to have him, but I wasn't the kind of person who needed to be constantly surrounded by other people in order to be happy. Not like Drew.

Which was why I needed to figure out a way to get Ryan out of my apartment and on his merry way through the afterlife.

"No, thanks," I said with a wink. "Girl stuff."

"Ah, 'nuff said!" He laughed as he backed away, hands up and palms out in surrender. "I don't want nor need details. I'll come get you for break."

"Thanks, Drew." I shot him a quick smile before grabbing my mail cart and wheeling it into the sorting room.

Nine hours later, I trudged up the three flights of stairs to my apartment, ready to kick off my shoes, take a long hot shower, and order takeout because I was too exhausted to walk down the street. And I wanted to do all of that in the comfort and privacy of my home.

Work had been nerve-wracking and I was done dealing with hateful, impatient, and overall unpleasant people for the day and didn't want to risk running into one more person intent on sucking the happiness from my soul.

But walking into my apartment, I remembered that privacy was a luxury I no longer had.

Ryan stood with his back against the wall, arms crossed over his chest, as he gazed out the window into open air.

"Honey, I'm home!" I called out jovially.

Ryan glanced over his shoulder. "Har-har, very funny."

I dropped my purse and keys onto the kitchen counter and flopped into a chair. "Well, I figured it was a better greeting than, 'oh great, you're still here.'"

"Where else would I be?" He sighed.

"Gee, I don't know, Heaven? The Summerland? Asphodel Meadows?"

Ryan's chest moved with a silent chuckle.

"Well, I'm not Wiccan, nor a follower of the Greek Gods, so no."

I nodded, surprised he'd understood those references. "Okay, so you're just gonna haunt a crappy, run-down apartment in Chinatown for all eternity?"

"God, I hope not."

"Yeah, that would be a fairly dismal way to spend the afterlife."

"Fairly dismal?" He asked, sending me a genuine smile flying over his shoulder.

"Well, it sure beats a fiery inferno of punishment and pain, does it not?"

He lowered his eyes as his smile vanished in an instant. "That it does, Mercy, that it does."

The room fell silent as he went back to staring out the window. His eyes held so much sadness that I found myself fighting the urge to cross the room and take him in my arms. I didn't know much about him, but he just didn't seem like he deserved this fate. I hated that he was in pain, and I hated that there wasn't a single thing I could do to fix it. Seeing people in undeserved agony was my Achilles heel.

I caught myself imagining the way I could tuck his shaggy hair behind his ear and tell him everything was going to be okay. I would nudge his shoulder and make a joke at my own expense just to see him crack a smile. Or I would tickle his sides until he bellowed out in raucous laughter.

Shaking my head, I banished those crazy thoughts. Yes, Ryan was attractive, and yes, he was hiding a funny, sharp, and compassionate side, I was sure of it. Add on top of that that he'd saved my butt

102

the night before, and I couldn't help but feel *something* for him.

But Ryan was operating on a whole other plane of existence. True, he was standing right before me, but he wasn't really there. He was alive in spirit, but dead in all other ways that were so important.

Joining him at the window, I crossed my arms so I wouldn't be tempted to reach out for him in his time of need. "What are you looking at?"

He let out a long breath, which I still found hard to understand since he didn't have *lungs,* but I guess some habits are hard to break. "I don't know. People living? Families laughing? Life going on without me?"

My eyes scanned the streets below until they landed on a homeless man sitting next to a coffee can with only a few quarters inside. "That guy doesn't seem to be laughing."

"Nope. And sadly, I think I have more in common with him than any other person walking those streets right now."

"That's not true. He looks so alone." Ryan closed his eyes, but I kept talking. "And you're not alone. You have a super cool roommate to keep you company."

Using the word 'roommate' was hilarious, since I felt like Ryan was intruding on my life in some way. But he looked so crestfallen, I had to at least attempt to make him feel better.

"Do I now?" He asked, cracking a smile. "Well, I think my roommate's trying to evict me."

I shook my head even though he still wasn't looking at me. "Maybe at first she was, but that's just because she was being a pansy. But then she thought, 'who am I to question life, to question existence?' No one, that's who. And I was raised to believe that there's a reason for everything. I don't always buy into that, but maybe it has some merit. Maybe there's a reason *you're* here."

"If there is, I wish someone would explain it to me."

"Maybe that someone is a little busy right now. Or, maybe you're supposed to meet them halfway. Or heck, maybe you're just supposed to figure it out on your own. After all, they say life's a journey, not a destination. Maybe you're still on your journey."

The more I talked, the cornier I sounded. I knew that, but I didn't bother to stop or correct myself. Maybe Ryan would find some semblance of humor to my words and it would drag him out of the depression he'd cocooned himself in.

Trying to read his tight expression, I watched Ryan's jaw clench as he fell deep into thought. Without his eyes on me, I was able to get a good look at him without feeling like he was staring straight through me, into the depths of my being. His blue eyes had a way of making me feel exposed- like he could see all my secrets. Like he knew me in a way I would never know myself.

Ryan was clearly young, in his early twenties, but the bags under his eyes made him seem so much older, frailer, like he hadn't slept soundly in months. Which was ridiculous, since he was dead. I always thought that the dead, if people could see them, would be restored to perfect health and would be the beautiful, flawless creatures they were meant to be before the weight of the world was placed on their shoulders. But Ryan looked human. He looked flawed. And he looked pained, exhausted, and beaten down. And that was partially my fault. But maybe I could remedy that.

"Ryan?"

"What?" His eyes remained closed.

"What were you like? In life, I mean."

His blue eyes finally snapped open as he tilted his head down to meet my gaze.

"Pretty much the same as I am now," he said softly. "Just a little less *dead*."

My heart shattered at his proclamation. He had to have been so much more. Surely his life had been filled with love and kindness and laughter. Deep down, I knew he was an elaborate being, someone who was worthy of so much more than being imprisoned in the space where he had breathed his last breath.

"C'mon." I nodded toward the couch. "Talk to me."

# Chapter Eight

## Ryan

When I was alive, I wouldn't have hesitated. I would have sat down on the couch next to Mercy and maybe even held her hand, brushed my knee against hers, or laid my arm across the back of the couch above her shoulders. As it was, I couldn't do any of those things, not even sit on the couch. The walls and floor seemed to be my prison bars, but everything else was just... luggage for the living.

"What's wrong?" She asked, noticing my hesitation.

I offered her a sardonic grin as I jerked my chin in the direction of the couch. "Haven't quite figured out furniture yet."

"Oh," she laughed. "Right. Sorry."

I picked a spot on the floor next to her feet and slumped down before resting my arms on my bent knees. "This is about as comfortable as it gets for me."

She nodded and began picking at the dark blue polish on her nails- a nervous tick, I'd come to realize. Her thin brows furrowed as she concentrated on a vacant spot on the floor. For a moment, all that could be heard was the ticking of the kitchen clock and the dull roar of the AC.

"Do you have any family?" She asked, ending the loaded silence.

"I do," I answered. "My parents and Quinn, my twin sister."

"Twin? That's cool. Are you two a lot alike?"

Talking about Quinn made me want to disappear, or drive a screwdriver into my chest to kill the emptiness that lingered there. But Mercy was being open and kind for once, and I couldn't let that slip away.

"In ways. We have, uh- had, that secret twin connection thing going on when we were younger. Used to freak our parents out when one of us would get hurt and the other would cry." I chuckled, remembering the time Quinn fell off her bike and I had sore knees for a week. "But that disappeared with age. We stayed close, but work and other obligations kept us from seeing each other as much as we liked."

"And your parents?" She asked.

"My parents," I said with a sigh. "Evelyn and Robert Callahan. Both workaholics. Both too busy and stressed out to ever notice what's going on around them."

"They sound pretty serious."

Mercy was listening, really listening, and

107

talking to someone felt too good to stop.

"Yeah, you could say that. They were pretty stern parents growing up, when they took time off to spend time with us anyway. All about the rules and being all you could be. My father was a real hard ass... pardon my French."

Her eyes flew to her lap as she fidgeted with the hem of her shirt. "Rules," she chuckled, "must have been nice."

"Since when are rules nice?" I asked. "Kids are supposed to hate rules."

"Maybe, but I wish my parents would have cared enough to set boundaries for me and my brother growing up. They're a little out there."

"Out there how?" I asked. I wanted to know more about her, more about who she was, where she came from, and what made her uniquely *her*.

"My parents are as hippie as you can get. You know, the whole free love, save the earth, your aura is muddied, don't eat that it's bad for you kind of people."

I couldn't picture Mercy coming from parents like that. She was so straight laced and clean. She didn't have tarot cards spread out across the kitchen counter or incense burning through the house. Aside from the handmade crafts littering the shelves, everything about her home was tidy and utilitarian, as was the way she carried herself.

"They sound groovy," I said, earning myself a smile.

"They sure think so."

"So what do they think of you living in the middle of a big city, ordering Chinese food in nonbiodegradable containers, working a nine-to-five job and owning a brain-scrambling cell phone?"

She stopped smiling and dropped her eyes to her lap. She pulled her bottom lip in between her teeth and chewed nervously as she struggled for an answer.

"Look, you don't have to talk about them if it's a sore subject. Trust me, I understand how difficult parents can be."

"Sore subject," she laughed. "Yeah, you could say that. They would probably have a complete meltdown if they could see how I'm living right now."

I looked around the apartment, at her simple but nice belongings and the tidiness of the place and scooted closer to her feet so she could see the sincerity in my eyes.

"Looks like you're doing pretty well for yourself. You're not snorting lines off the coffee table or advertising a red light special out your window. They should be proud."

Her lips twitched to the side, squelching a grin as she looked around the apartment herself.

"Yeah... they should be."

As she continued to look around, I couldn't help but stare. Her light blue eyes had flecks of green I hadn't noticed before. Her high cheek bones and dainty nose gave her a pixie quality which was only accented by the wide curve of her full bottom lip. Add to that her complete lack of makeup and she was perfect. She was beautiful in a subtle way most women dreamed of being.

"So, are you from Chicago?"

I pulled my eyes away from her lips to find her smiling again. Not a friendly smile. The kind of smile women give men when they catch them doing something boorish. She'd caught me.

"Uh, yeah. Lived here all my life."

"You've never lived anywhere else?" She sounded surprised.

"Nope. I was born in the Windy City and I died in the Windy City. I did a little bit of traveling, but this has always been my home."

She huffed out a laugh before offering me one of her rare smiles I was starting to enjoy a little too much. "That must have been awesome. My parents dragged me all over the continental U.S. I don't think we ever stayed in one spot for more than a year. Sometimes I was lucky and could stay in the same school district, but we flipped homes constantly. My parents thrive on instability."

"And you?" I asked, anxious to know more about her. "What do you thrive on?"

She tilted her head to the side and fiddled with the ends of her hair, narrowing her eyes at the wall as she contemplated her answer. "I'm not sure. I mean, I don't think I've really had the chance to thrive yet, so there's no telling. But I *do* know that I hate the way my parents live. I don't want that. I want stability and consistency and normalcy." She shrugged shyly. "I want the American dream."

"Boring job, 401k, Range Rover, husband, kids, a white picket fence... that American dream?"

"Yup," she grinned as she laced her fingers together on her lap. "That's the one."

"I'd say you're on the right track."

"And you?" She asked quietly. "What did you want out of life?"

I sighed heavily, dropping my head into my hands and threading my fingers through my coarse, brown hair. What a loaded question. I remembered wanting things, and that was the worst part of my life being cut short. Everything I'd ever wanted no longer mattered. For Mercy, the sky was the limit, the possibilities were endless. But for me? This was it.

"Nothing I managed to acquire," I finally answered.

I couldn't tell Mercy that I had wanted the same things. For one, she would take pity on me because my life was over and none of that stuff mattered anymore. But also, because I didn't want her to feel guilty, and she struck me as the kind of girl who would feel bad about having something when someone else had to go without.

"Tell me about your sister, Quinn." Mercy said, pulling me back into the conversation. "When was the last time you two saw each other?"

"Uh, Christmas, I think. Yeah, we spent Christmas Eve with our parents. But I've seen her since then." Mercy shook her head like she didn't understand. "Mrs. Whitlock boxed up all my things so Quinn wouldn't have to do it. I watched her load up the boxes," I pointed at the window, my only connection to the outside world. "She's a trooper. Didn't shed a single tear until she drove away."

"Sounds like a family trait," Mercy said with a smile.

"What is?"

"Being strong. Keeping it together."

I caught Mercy's gaze and held it. I prayed she wouldn't blink as I drew closer, trying to comprehend the rare sentiment in her eyes. But as soon as a blush began creeping up her neck, she turned away.

She thought I was strong? Why? I was dead... I couldn't *be* strong. That particular attribute was a hop, skip, and a jump out of the circle of things I was allowed to be.

"So, what about your brother?" I asked in hopes of keeping the conversation alive.

"Lyric is everything you'd expect a big brother to be. Annoying, intrusive, bullheaded... but I love him, and he's always been there for me when I needed him."

"Is he like you? A hippie-hater?"

She scoffed. "Absolutely not. He's actually worse than my parents. Lyric is a nomad, so he's pretty much a hippie with no home whatsoever. He just... wanders around the world." She shuddered like the idea repulsed her. "I don't know how he does it. I would feel so lost all the time."

"Maybe that's why he does it. Maybe he is lost, but he's trying to find himself."

"Oh God," she laughed. "You're starting to sound like my family."

"Hey, man," I drawled, doing my best stoner impression. "You've just gotta bring the peace, man. Your aura's bringin' me down."

Mercy cackled. "You do that *way* too well."

"I feel the need... to speak with the trees," I crossed my legs and pressed my fingers to my temples as Mercy grew breathless with laughter. "The oaks are telling me that the dolphins are crying in the sea because the entire system is corrupt."

"Seriously, stop that!" She fanned her face as

she tried to stop laughing. "You're freaking me out."

"I'm freakin' you out, man? You just need to mellow out."

"Ryan," she giggled "Stop that."

Then she did something I wasn't expecting, something I couldn't stop. She leaned forward, aiming to give me a playful nudge on the shoulder, but lost her balance when her hand met air and before I knew it, she was sprawled across the floor.

"Oh my God! Are you okay?"

Mercy's laughter died away as she pushed herself off the ground and sat on the edge of the couch, tucking a lock of hair behind her ear as she blushed.

"Just... forgot there for a second," she said sadly.

And just like that, because of her sadness, I couldn't look at her. I couldn't look at her because she wasn't sad out of pity. She was truly sad, not for my sake, but for her own. She was sad, because for one brief moment I had made her happy. For a moment, I made her smile. And when the shocking reality of the situation was laid at her feet, it stung. She was alive. I was dead. Nothing short of existence and infinity separated us.

"I should probably start getting ready for bed," she said quietly.

I nodded. "Right. Yeah, I'll, uh, I'll let you do that."

"'Kay." She stood and made her way to the bathroom. "Goodnight, Ryan."

As she turned her blue eyes on me one last time before stepping through the door, I fought against the selfish need to tell her to stay, to keep talking, keep laughing with me. But I addressed her with a closed-mouth smile to keep my pleas to myself.

I'd already taken up too much of her time, and she had better things to do than spend hours conversing with the dead. Luckily, the part of me that wanted her to stay was easily silenced, but only because even though the night had ended badly, I knew there would be more nights like this to come.

"Goodnight, Mercy."

# Mercy

Through the next few nights, Ryan was quiet. Standoffish. Brooding. Of course, it had everything to do with my clumsy display of forgetfulness. Just when he was beginning to come out of his shell, one move from me sent him running. I'd tried to engage him in conversation, but his heart wasn't in it. He just kept staring out that stupid window, like the answers to life were going to appear in skywriting. Or he was doing it to distance himself from me.

"Running," I grumbled to myself as I trudged up the stairs. "Like he can get any farther away."

"Are you talking to yourself?"

I whipped my head up to find a surprise leaning against my front door.

"Lyric! What are you doing here?" I ran to my big brother and thew my arms around his shoulders. Different or not- we were blood, I loved him, and there was no one else on the planet who I wanted to see more. "How'd you find my place?"

"Got Drew's number from mom and dad."

"Figures," I playfully punched him in the arm. "I can't believe you're here! How was Manitou Springs? We didn't really get to talk last time I called home, at least not about your latest adventure."

"It was exquisite, Mercy. Rainbow Falls just blew me away. The shots I got were some of my best. Should be easy to sell once they're printed and framed. And I met some really nice people there that let me crash with them. All in all, the trip was one of my favorites. I really wish you could have been there."

"One of these days I'll join you on one of your epic quests," I assured him.

"I hope so."

"You know, Chicago has some pretty great sites as well. Why don't you stay with me for a while and you can wander the city and do some shoots while I'm at work."

"I don't know, sis." He cringed in that unique way of his and I knew he wasn't even considering it.

"Awe, c'mon! You've been on the road for so long. Wouldn't it be nice to just chill out for a while? A few weeks? Maybe longer?"

"To you maybe, but that's not me, Mercy, and you know it."

"I also know that your lifestyle worries me. Look at you, bub! I've seen cleaner homeless people digging through the dumpsters out back."

He laughed as he pushed a hand through his shoulder length brown hair. His clothes were dusty, his boots a little too worn, and judging from his posture, he was exhausted.

"I would tell you what you keep telling mom

and dad -that my life is none of your business- but I have a feeling it would go in one ear and out the other."

"And you'd be right." I poked him in the chest for emphasis.

"I thought I was supposed to look after *you,* baby sister. I don't need you fretting over me."

"Can't look after someone who's bouncing from state to state every few days," I said with a wink. "If you'd sit still for more than a week, you'd bet your Canon I'd be keeping tabs on you."

He raised his hands and nodded. "Okay, *mother.* Now, can we go inside and see this apartment that has mom and dad in knots?"

"Of course." I unlocked the door and gestured for Lyric to go in ahead of me.

"It's a little small," he said, even as he nodded in approval, "but cozy. Really cozy."

"Thanks," I beamed. I was proud of what I'd done with the place. "Want something to drink? I have lemonade and tea."

"Sounds good," he answered.

Since we were children, his favorite drink had always been organic lemonade mixed with freshly brewed iced tea. I'd heard people refer to the mixture as an 'Arnold Palmer', but I had no idea why.

I skipped to the kitchen, overjoyed by my big brother's surprise visit, and gasped when I found Ryan perched on a bar stool.

"Didn't know we were having company."

Pulling my thumb and pointer finger across my lips, I gestured for Ryan to zip it. I didn't need Lyric knowing about Ryan. My brother was just as

117

sensitive and intuitive as I was, and if I could see, hear, and feel Ryan's presence, so could he.

"Oh, I'm not supposed to exist today? Got it."

I shook my head but went about making drinks. Taking down two mismatched tumblers, I sat them on the counter next to where Ryan stood and carefully skirted my eyes around his form while I retrieved the lemonade and tea from the fridge.

"Gonna ignore me the whole time he's here?"

Peeking out the corner of my eye, refusing to give him the satisfaction of looking him head on, I could see that Ryan was fuming.

"What's wrong with you? Why are you so angry?" I whispered.

"Angry? Aw, no, I'm not angry. I love not existing. I love it when people look right through me. It's a great feeling, really."

"Need any help?" Lyric asked from the living room.

"Uh, no! I've got it. Just gimme a sec." I relented long enough to turn pleading eyes to Ryan, who looked like he was about to spit bullets. "Can you please stay in here until he leaves? I know that's a horrible thing to ask, but... please?"

He didn't answer, but he also didn't move, so I took that as a sign of compliance.

"Sorry," I whispered as I left the kitchen.

"You really should have thought twice about inviting me to stay with you," Lyric said as he walked around the tiny space. "There's not enough room for roaches in here, let along another human being."

"You'd be surprised," I muttered.

"What was that?"

118

"Nothing. Here," I handed him a glass. "The lemonade's not organic and the tea isn't fresh, but it's cold."

"Thanks." He took a sip before placing it on the coffee table and taking a seat. "So, new city, new apartment, new job, what else is new?"

My phone chirped from within my purse and I reached over to check it without thinking.

"Ah, that's new. So I take it you've completely crossed over to the dark side."

"You try operating in a strange city without a phone."

"I do," he pointed out. "Every day."

"Well, you're not me."

"Obviously. I'm not the heretic."

"Very funny," I said, taking a seat next to him. "So, what's new with you? Where do you go from here?"

"I'm not sure," he said, stretching out on the couch. "But I've got big things happening in my life."

"Oh yeah?" I asked. "New commission?"

"Nope. I went to visit Sister Faye."

I groaned. "Oh God, you have *got* to be kidding me. That crazy old fortune teller does nothing but read up on people and take their money. Nothing she says is ever accurate and it's always so vague it could be taken a million different ways. I can't believe you've sunk so much money into that old hag. Really, you think you'd know better by-"

"She said!" He yelled, cutting me off. "That I'm to father a dove."

Quietly, I let that sink in. As it did, I had to bite my lip just to keep from laughing."A dove?" I asked. "You're going to father a bird?"

"Not that kind of dove," he said, kicking my shin. "A dove is another word for peacemaker."

"Uh huh... and what is this dove going to bring peace to?"

He was silent for a few beats, before taking a deep breath and saying, "Our family."

"Our family? I wasn't aware we were at war."

"Whatever," he sighed before crossing his arms. "I knew you wouldn't understand."

"What I understand is that you're being jipped out of your hard-earned money! And besides, you haven't even had a girlfriend since the eleventh grade because you're never in one spot long enough to start a relationship. So, how are you going to father this great peace-monger? Immaculate conception?"

"For the record, you don't have to be in a relationship to have a kid, just FYI."

"Oh, I see how you're working it. You're just gonna bed women from city to city until you get a call that your dove has hatched, is that it?"

"Can we just drop this and have a decent visit," Lyric finally snapped. "Please?"

I heaved out a frustrated sigh and picked up my drink. "Fine."

We sat in silence, neither of us making a move to talk in fear of sparking another fight. We would never see eye to eye, that was crystal clear. In a way, I guess Lyric was right. Our family was at war. Not on a grand scale by any means, but there was definitely an unrest, a fission, between the members of our tribe. But it wasn't something I was going to lose sleep over.

"Whew, it just got cold in here."

My head fell back with a groan and I turned to see Ryan, arms crossed over his chest, head tilted to the side, eying Lyric. I shook my head as he inched closer to my brother under the guise of taking his normal spot by the window.

"Seriously, it's freezing in here."

"Hang on, I'll go check the thermostat in my room. Maybe it's broken." I shot up from the couch and jerked my chin in the direction of my bedroom and Ryan stoically followed.

"What are you doing?" I whisper-shouted as soon as we rounded the corner.

"Who is that guy, anyway? Does he ever bathe?"

"Why does it matter?"

"Uh, because bathing is important? He looks like he just climbed out of a-"

"No!" I waved my hands in the air to silence him. "I mean why do you care who he is?"

"Curiosity."

I crossed my arms and leaned back against the wall. "I would warn you about curiosity killing the cat, but I think we're a little past that."

Hurt flashed across Ryan's eyes and his jaw clenched as he turned his back to me. However, that was short lived. He spun on his heel, jutting a finger in the direction of Lyric before he lashed out. "I'm just looking out for you! That guy has done nothing but judge you since the second you walked through the door. Why on earth would you invite him here if he was going to treat you like that? Do you make it a habit to surround yourself with jerks? Because you don't deserve that."

Aside from the pain caused by my snide remark, there was something else in his voice, something I never expected. "Oh my God! You're jealous."

"What?" He whipped his head back in surprise. "No! That... that's insane. I'm not jealous."

"Yes, you are. You're jealous because I have a guy in my apartment. A living, breathing man that looks right through you like you don't exist. Because you don't!"

"That's a little harsh, don't you think?" His voice fell cold and dispassionate along with his eyes.

"No, I don't, because you being jealous is completely, one-hundred percent, off the charts ridiculous." A tension headache was quickly hacking it's way into my skull and I had to pinch the bridge of my nose and breathe in a deep, calming breath to keep from losing my cool. "That *jerk* is Lyric. That's my brother, Ryan."

At Ryan's stricken and abashed expression, I strode from the room, eager to end that particularly uncomfortable conversation. What was Ryan thinking, lashing out like that? And more so, why did I find it oddly flattering that he was so passionate about who I spent my time with?

"Fixed it!" I rejoined Lyric, only to find him grimacing as he scrolled through my phone.

"Why are you so opposed to me carrying around that little piece of technology?" I asked, taking a seat beside him. "It's just a phone. Just a way to communicate with my friends. Why do you look so mad?"

"I'm not mad about you having a phone. I'm

mad because you have the damn thing and you haven't bothered to call mom and dad. Not once. They miss you, Mercy! It's killing them that you don't write, you don't call, you haven't gone back to see them. You've just disappeared from their lives."

"I haven't even been gone a month! They haven't even had time to miss me yet. And it's not like *you're* not off doing your own thing."

"Yeah, I am," he shot back, "but I still check in with them every other day."

"Why? And why on earth would *I* do that? I haven't done a single thing since I've gotten here that warrants a call home. I've done nothing."

"They don't expect you to have a neat little progress report printed out. They just want to talk to their daughter. They want to know how you're doing, tell you they love you. We've always been close, so you pulling out of the family was a bit of a shock for them, alright? You have to give them time to acclimate to the change." His head fell forward as my phone clattered to the coffee table. "Just... ease their worries. Call them. Is that too much to ask?"

It was. It really was. Lyric couldn't and wouldn't understand what I was trying to do in Chicago. He didn't understand why I left and why I swore never to go back to that way of life. No, I didn't hate my parents and I didn't see my move as running away from their love or abandoning my family. I just needed space until I sorted myself out. Until I made something of myself.

"I'm trying to distance myself from their life, Lyric," I whispered, hoping he would listen if I lowered my verbal fists. "I'm sorry that I'm distancing myself from them in the process, but that's just part of it. That's just how it is. And I wish you could understand that."

With a cynical laugh, Lyric rose to his feet and headed for the door. I reached out to stop him, but he pulled away and was at the door before I could stand.

"I get that you want to be your own kind of person, and I respect that. But no matter how far you go, no matter what kind of clothes you wear or how much nasty, unnatural food you eat... they're still going to love you. They're still going to want you in their lives. And you're still going to be their daughter. They set your heart to beating- don't you ever forget that. So grow up, quit being a brat, and show some respect."

The door slammed shut behind him and I was left feeling like my favorite person on earth had just sucker punched me in the gut.

His words hurt. A lot.

I stood in the middle of the empty living room, fighting tears as I debated whether or not to go after him. My feet moved toward the door, but my mind stopped them in their tracks. There was nothing I could say to Lyric. Every word he spoke, no matter how deep it sliced me, had been true. I was a brat. A brat who thought she knew better than her parents. A brat who took her entire childhood for granted and pushed away all the people who loved her most.

Instead of going after him, I picked his half-empty glass off the table, slunk to the kitchen, and dropped it in the sink.

Bracing both hands against the counter, I replayed our conversation over and over in my head

124

until my heart ached.

"God, I'm an awful person."

When I could no longer fight the tears, I made my way to my bedroom. I deserved to cry. I deserved to feel like my heart was being pulled inside-out. Because Lyric was right, our family was at war. And I'd fired the first shot. For every pinprick of pain I'd ever caused my family, I deserved the blowback tenfold.

Ryan reached out for me as I passed, but I stepped out of reach as his hand halted in mid-air. Without saying a word, he dropped his hand and turned to face the window with a sadness that sucked every degree of heat from the room. I hated myself for cringing away from him when he was only trying to console me, but I didn't deserve solace. Not the least little bit.

# Chapter Nine

## Ryan

That was stupid. Incredibly. Freaking. Stupid.

I had no right to feel *anything* toward Mercy, let alone jealousy. I knew I'd never have any kind of claim to her whatsoever. Hell, I couldn't even have a real connection with her. But I couldn't help but think about her every moment of every day. I couldn't help *wanting* to spend time with her, no matter how bleak I knew the outcome to be. But, like a lovesick teenager, I couldn't help myself. I couldn't help but be drawn to her and all her quirky, confident, effervescent splendor.

"Well... that could have gone better."

I didn't bother turning to face Willa, but I could tell from her voice that she was smiling at my predicament.

"You know, I could be haunting someone who

126

wronged me in life," I said. "I could be out seeing the world, discovering the secrets of the universe, but instead, I'm spending my days smiling about a woman I barely know and can never have. Is that completely pathetic?"

"Yes. It is."

"Wow. Don't sugar coat it for me. Tell me what you really think," I deadpanned.

The bedroom door opened and Willa and I both turned to watch Mercy carry a change of clothes, her radio, and a towel into the bathroom with her. She didn't even acknowledge my existence as she walked through the room, empty-eyed and dejected.

"Don't you think you're being a little overly dramatic?" Willa asked after the door closed and locked behind Mercy.

"Of course I think that."

"Then stop. Refocus your energy on something healthier, something less... adolescent."

"Adolescent," I laughed. "This coming from a pre-pubescent girl with flowers in her hair?"

We both glanced at the closed bathroom door as music blared through the thin wood paneling. Whatever had gone down between Mercy and her brother had deeply upset her, and it was showing.

"Speaking of adolescent," Willa said, cringing at Mercy's choice of music.

I nodded along with the beat, mouthing the words to the angsty boy band anthem.

"Seriously?" Willa laughed.

"Quinn used to love this song," I said, remembering the ridiculous posters Quinn had plastered all over her bedroom walls. It would figure

127

that Mercy would have the same taste in music as my sister.

"This is awful. I actually had Mercy pegged as more of a classical girl. You know- Mozart, Beethoven, Haydn."

"Nah. That girl needs words. She needs to sing."

"Wow, you've got it bad."

Willa was smiling, but it was stiff, unconvincing.

"What's wrong with you?"

"Aside from having to put up with you crushing all over Mrs. Boring over there?" She threw a thumb over her shoulder, gesturing to the bathroom.

"Boring? Mercy is the complete opposite of boring, okay? She's one of the most interesting, genuine, and true people I've ever met. Both in life *and* in death."

"Ouch," Willa slapped a hand over her heart before stumbling backwards. "That hurt."

"Sorry," I grinned. "You come in a close second if that makes you feel any better."

"Aww, so sweet. Aren't you a charmer? Way to make a girl feel..." Willa trailed off as her eyes grew dense with worry.

"What? What's the matter?"

"Do you smell that?" She asked, tilting her nose in the air and taking a big whiff like a seasoned hunting dog.

"I'm dead, Willa. I can't smell anyth-" My non-existent heart stuttered as a plume of smoke wafted up from beneath the door.

I was at the bathroom door in two steps,

screaming for Mercy at the top of my lungs.

"Mercy! Mercy, get out here!"

"She can't hear you!" Willa shouted. "Get in there!"

"I don't know how!"

"Ugh, do I have to do everything myself?"

Before I could ask what that meant, Willa put both hands on my back and shoved. Sparks flew from her palms and into my spine as I cried out and arched against the pain. But there was no time to worry about my own discomfort.

"Mercy! There's a fire! Get out here!"

The godawful music still drowned out my voice and I turned back to Willa for help.

"You have to get her attention!" She yelled. "Just jump in!"

"What? I can't do that!"

Willa rolled her eyes. "I'm sure she'll thank you for keeping her dignity intact after she burns to death in a fire. Do something!"

Refusing to intrude on Mercy any more than I already had, I frantically searched the cluttered bathroom for anything that could help me get her attention.

The radio was already at max volume, so my parlor trick with that wouldn't work. The blow dryer? No, I wanted to get her attention, not accidentally electrocute her...

"The water!" Willa yelled, jumping up and down as she pointed.

Without a second thought, I stuck my hand in between the wall and the shower curtain and straight into the stream of hot water, turning it ice cold as it sprayed through my essence.

Mercy screamed to high heaven before turning the water off and poking her head around the curtain.

"What are you DOING?"

"Fire," I yelled, pointing at the door. "You have to get out of here. Now!"

Mercy's blue eyes went wide at the sight of smoke fluttering in under the door. Before she could ask, I turned my back and listened as she threw on her clothes, jerked the stereo cord out of the wall, and lurched for the door.

# Mercy

As my heart thundered away at two hundred miles an hour within my chest, I dropped to the ground where the air was clearer and made my way through my apartment. Tenants were pouring out of their doors, coughing, crying, and screaming orders to their family and friends as everyone flooded to the exits. Surprisingly, we all made it out the door, down the stairwell, and out to the street in record time.

I went from group to group, trying to figure out what was happening. All I could tell was that the building had begun filling with smoke, but no one had actually seen flames and the fire alarm hadn't sounded.

"We just happened to smell it," a young Chinese man said in a heavily accented voice. "I thought Mary was just burning dinner."

"Could you tell where it was coming from?" Another nameless person asked.

"Somewhere on the third floor. That's all we could tell."

I kept walking, my mind whirling through a million different scenarios and outcomes. I wouldn't have been able to smell the smoke while I was in the shower with my potent shampoo. I wouldn't have been able to tell smoke from steam from the hot water. I wouldn't have heard the screams over the volume of my radio.

But I'd still made it out.

Thanks to Ryan.

Weaving through the other coughing tenants on the street, I searched for and found Alice. She was consoling a family of five as their children wept on the street.

"Alice," I said, grabbing her arm. "What happened?"

"Oh, there you are!" She yelled, taking me into her arms. "You're the last of them."

The wailing of sirens pierced through the night air as two firetrucks turned the corner and headed our way.

"Help me get everyone out of the way!" Alice barked.

Each and every tenant spent the next hour watching the firemen work, coughing and sputtering and praying for their homes to be saved. Some of the area businesses offered to open their lobbies and get us off the streets, but there's just something about a fire that draws people in. Even though we couldn't see flames, we had to be in the center of the action. Curious eyes bounced from the door to the firemen to the third floor windows, and occasionally strayed to other tenants.

But me? My eyes never left the window of

Apartment thirty-three. Through the smoke, I could make out Ryan's silhouette as he stood with his arms crossed, watching over me. Protecting me.

Saving me.

Despite the fact that the entire building had filled with smoke, the fire damage was minimal. Someone had fallen asleep with a cigarette in their hand and caught the carpet on fire. It had taken the firefighters seconds to put it out, but we weren't allowed back in until they were sure everything was sound and protocol was met.

Shortly after midnight, I hugged a worried Alice in the lobby before heading up to see what kind of smoke damage I had to deal with.

"No one was hurt," I assured her. "That's all that matters."

"I suppose you're right. I just can't help worrying that-"

"Stop that!" I grabbed her by the shoulders and pulled her in for a hug. She looked like she could use one. "It's just smoke damage and a room of carpet burnt to a crisp. It could have been a lot worse."

Alice hugged me back before pulling away. I couldn't tell if the tears in her eyes were from the residual smoke or the emotion bubbling up her throat.

"Thank you, dear." She smoothed a hand over her blouse and gestured for me to head upstairs.

"Get some sleep, okay? Promise me."

"I promise, Mercy." Her smile was paired with a shake of her head, no doubt due to the idea of someone fifty years her junior bossing her around.

I started up the stairs, more than ready to crash

for the night now that the adrenaline had drained from my system. My legs felt like lead cylinders as I trudged up all three flights. Arriving at my door, I found I'd neglected to pull it closed in my haste to escape.

Pushing my way inside, I expected to find soot covered walls and windows, but everything was as I left it. Not even a puff of smoke lingered in the air. My eyes bounced from floor to ceiling, wall to wall, taking in the simple perfection of my apartment before turning to face Ryan. Our eyes collided as he flicked his gaze over one shoulder. A cold, haunted look marred his usually pensive, yet handsome face.

"Hey."

"You okay?" He asked.

"Not a scratch."

I crossed the floor, swallowing around the lump in my throat as I fought to find the words to thank Ryan. Again.

"Look, I'm not very good at this, so my apologies almost always suck, but I'm really sorry about earlier. I shouldn't have yelled at you."

Ryan turned back around to face the window. His broad shoulders hunched forward, his head bowed so that his chin rested just above his chest. But he didn't speak a word.

"It wasn't right for me to go off on you like that and I'm sorry." I figured backing up an apology with gratitude was the way to go. "And thank you, again, for what you did."

"Is this it, Mercy?" Ryan whispered, keeping his back to me. Something about his tone was different. More resigned. Like he'd completely given up.

"Is this what?" I shook my head, not understanding the question.

"Is this my job now? Is this what I'll spend eternity doing?" His voice grew louder. "Saving a naive woman because she can't save herself?

"Naive? Being in the shower while there's a freaking fire raging next door doesn't make me naive. And neither does being asleep when someone tries to rob my apartment. It makes me a victim of circumstance."

He turned and barreled toward me, anger and hurt warring for the spotlight in his eyes. "Do you have some kind of storm cloud that follows you around? Did some pissed off shaman sprinkle you with a curse when you were a baby? Because since the moment you walked through that door you've been nothing but one huge heaping pile of trouble. And apparently I've been assigned to be your babysitter, which is really starting to piss me off. There are a million other things I'd rather be doing than saving your ass, Mercy!"

"Stop yelling! You can't blame that on me. It's not like I *asked* for you to stay behind. I didn't even know you!"

"No, you didn't!" He howled. "Which is why this is so damn cruel!"

"What is?" I had absolutely no idea what he was talking about.

"This," he gestured between our bodies. "Being here, with you, all the damn time. Talking with you. Laughing with you. Watching over you..." His voice cracked as he took the last step between us, closing the distance as he held his hands next to my face. "But not being able to touch you. Or hug you. Or kiss you. I can't help but think this is some kind of punishment. And I don't know what in the hell I did in life to deserve this, but it had to be atrocious."

Ryan's eyes flickered back and forth between mine, searching for an answer I didn't have to give. And as his frustration grew, my chest ached with all the things I couldn't, shouldn't, and wouldn't say to him to ease his suffering. I had no words to ease his pain. No salve that could heal his wounds. Because I'd begun to do the unthinkable, and if I continued down that road, it would be the end for both of us.

Ryan eventually turned away when he realized I had nothing to say.

"If you don't mind," he said, "I think I need some time to myself."

"You- you want me to leave?" I croaked. He couldn't kick me out of my own apartment, but if he wanted me to leave, I would. I'd give him that much.

"No. I just want... God, what do I want?"

He fell silent, brooding over who knows what.

I knew what he wanted, what had been taken from him much too soon.

And I wanted it just as badly.

# Chapter Ten

# Ryan

I wanted my feelings for Mercy to disappear. They had enveloped me, latched themselves to me like a skin graph. At first, she had just been a face. Just a pretty girl out of my reach. But after spending time with her, watching her, and learning all there was to know about the enigmatic Mercy Hunter, I found myself cursing how unfair both life and death had been to me. My feelings for her had exploded out of nowhere, and there was no way to escape the burn.

I didn't want to love her. Surely I couldn't love her in just the short amount of time we'd spent together. Maybe it was just infatuation. Or... maybe we were kindred spirits, and I was *chosen* to stay behind for Mercy.

*That's ridiculous, Ryan. What kind of deity would be that cruel?*

And it was cruel. It was cruel the way I wondered what it would be like to touch her face or feel her breath on my skin in that moment before a kiss. And envisioning a life with her? That was the epitome of cruelty.

But the saddest thing was that the cruelty was *worth* it. It was worth staying behind. It was worth being with Mercy. She made me feel... less dead. And I didn't have the willpower to stay away.

So, when she tucked herself into bed, I found myself standing at her bedroom window, inches away from where she rested.

"That wasn't fair, what I said before," I started. "And what your brother said earlier, before he left? That wasn't fair either. But what I said about you surrounding yourself with jerks? I think that was spot on, don't you? You keep putting your faith in people who don't deserve it, and they keep letting you down, myself included."

Toying with the edge of a fraying blanket, she shifted her eyes through the darkness until they collided with mine. Her eyebrows drew together as she opened her mouth, but she snapped her lips shut before she could speak.

"What is it, Mercy?"

She hesitated another second before closing her eyes and speaking. "Can I ask you something? Without hurting you?"

"I'm not sure," I answered honestly. "But you can try."

I watched her slim throat flex as she swallowed nervously.

"What's it feel like to be dead?" She asked in a

voice so small a passing car below drowned her out. But I heard her. Loud and clear.

Struggling, I fought back my own insecurities in order to give her a straight answer. The worry lines creasing her forehead told me that whatever answer I gave her she would take to heart. So, I answered with an abundance of honesty.

"You know that sensation you get right as you're waking up? That groggy uncertainty of not having a firm grasp on your body or your mind? That moment of disconnect right before you open your eyes?" I paused to let my words wash over her. "It feels like that. Magnified by a billion."

She nodded, as if that all made perfect sense.

"So... does it feel like there's something more?" She waved her arm through the air, gesturing to the apartment walls. "More than this?"

I shook my head, repulsed by the thought of this being *it*, but also put off by the thought of ever leaving Mercy. "I don't know."

"I hope there is," she said. "Because if not, what's the point? You know?"

"I ask myself that question every single day."

"And have you found an answer?"

"No," I said flatly. "Not yet. But sometimes I think I'm close."

She propped her head on her hand and turned her body to face me, eyes shining from the glow of streetlights below. "And when you do figure it out?"

"You'll be the first to know. I promise."

Smiling the saddest of smiles, Mercy nodded and rolled onto her back, snuggling into the comfort of her mattress.

"You've had a rough night. You should get some sleep," I said.

"You've had a rough afterlife. Maybe *you* should get some sleep."

Through the darkness, I watched her smile. In the quiet room, just the two of us, I knew that smile was meant just for me. That revelation alone pulled me out of my self-pity and into the glowing circle of Mercy's never-ending ability to make me feel like I mattered. Maybe being sent to watch over Mercy wasn't cruel at all.

Maybe it was a blessing.

# Mercy

At work the next day, even though every person sitting within a cubicle glared at me, I couldn't help but smile. Things were definitely rocky between Ryan and I, and my heart hurt in ways it never had before because of what had been taken from him. But he was opening up to me and, piece by piece, I was unearthing what kind of man he'd been in life. And from what I could see, he had been spectacular. He still was. Which is why I couldn't wipe the smirk off my face.

"You're awful perky this morning," Drew said as I wheeled my mail cart into the sorting room.

"She is, isn't she," Kayla, my boss, commented as she twirled a lock of short red hair around her finger.

Drew stood, hands on his hips, head cocked to the side as he gave me the once over. "Smiling, humming, a bounce in your step. What gives?"

"I think she's met someone," Kayla said in a sing-song voice.

"Really?" Drew smiled, waiting for me to dish the goods.

"What?" I squeaked. "No! I mean... not really. No."

"I call B.S." Kayla leaned over my cart and stared into my eyes. "You have *those* eyes."

"What eyes?" Drew asked, squinting to better see my face.

"Swoony eyes," she stated. "The eyes of someone who's falling in love."

*Love?*

No. I refused to think about that word, let alone what it could mean.

"See that?" Kayla pointed to my face before throwing a pointed glance at Drew. "That fear, that insecurity? That's her figuring it out. Don't fight it, sweetie. Just let it *be*."

They were so clueless. I couldn't just let it *be*. Because it could never be. It could never come to fruition. Because if there's one thing I knew, one thing I'd spent so many nights pondering over as I feigned sleep while Ryan was in the other room, it was this: Losing someone you love would be tragic. But falling in love with someone who's already dead would be an exquisite pain for which there was no remedy.

*Love? Do I love Ryan? Is that even possible?*
*No. It isn't. It's sick, even.*
*And yet...*

I thought about Ryan's eyes. The sadness they held and how I wanted nothing more than to reach out to him and assure him that everything was going to be okay, that I wasn't going anywhere. I thought of how I rushed home to see him everyday. I thought of all the questions I wanted to ask him, just so I could better understand the beauty of his existence and the man he was only just becoming. And then I thought of the ways he'd saved me.

I didn't know whether to laugh at the giddy feeling rising in my gut or cry and wallow at the injustices of the world. Either way, I couldn't be trusted to be close to my friends who, much to my dismay, could read me like a blind man reads braille. So, completely pushing Drew and Kayla from my mind, I wheeled my cart back out to the hall, took in a deep breath, and strode on, hating life and all the complexities it had decided to dump on my doorstep.

Sulking all the way home, I ran through everything I knew to be true about love. I had never experienced it first hand, but I knew a few things. It was all-consuming. It had no beginning and no end. It was kind and accepting and swept you into something more than yourself. It was... irrational.

*There's an enormous difference between irrational and physically impossible,* I told myself.

And yet, I couldn't help but want that. With Ryan. If I was one of those girls that concocted a list of traits required for her perfect man, Ryan would, without a doubt, be able to check off every last attribute. From his deadpan sense of humor to his rare smile. From his goofy hippie impersonations to the look of admiration that crossed his face when he talked about Quinn or Mrs. Whitlock. From the way he stared at me like he knew something I didn't to the way he turned his back when I needed a moment of privacy. Ryan was just... *perfect.* Which, in turn, made the entire situation a cruel and unusual form of punishment.

Dragging my feet through the hall, I paused in front of my apartment door, not quite ready to face Ryan after my drawn out, painful epiphany. Because that epiphany was absolutely absurd.

I had feelings for someone who was completely unattainable. And not in the normal rom-com, it's-complicated, Romeo-and-Juliet kind of way. He wasn't just in a different social class, or stationed across the globe. He wasn't a crush who didn't know my name or someone I admired from afar.

He was gone. Empty. *Dead.* The spark that defines us as human beings had been snuffed out and everything that remained of him was a shadow. And shadows can't feel. They can't embrace you, they can't dry your tears, they can't promise you a future. A shadow is just a void between light and reality.

Pulling in an unsteady breath, I squared my shoulders, plastered on a smile, and juggled the takeout containers in my hand as I fumbled my keys into the lock. Kicking open the door, I found the object of my confusion waiting at the window with a welcoming smile.

"Hey."

"Hey yourself," I kicked the door shut behind me and fought to keep my insides from turning to mush.

"How was your day?" He followed me into the kitchen where I unloaded my dinner. It was all so bizarre. Normal, yet not.

"Same stuff, different day."

"Sounds about right." He propped himself

against the wall, glancing between me and the window.

The way he made sure to look back and forth, like I might vanish or he might miss something outside, confused me to no end. All he did, day after day (apart from spending time with me) was stare out the windows. No matter what room he was in, he was always keeping watch over the city street. I wasn't sure why, and I didn't have it in me to ask in fear of not liking the answer.

Humming in appreciation, I closed my eyes and inhaled the steam rolling off my lo mein. Using chopsticks, I quickly emptied half the container onto my plate as my stomach set to rumbling.

Ryan chuckled even as he eyed my food with a hunger of a man who hadn't eaten for weeks. "Skip lunch again?"

"Yeah." I tossed one perfectly seasoned noodle into my mouth. "I didn't feel like going to the break room."

"That looks amazing," he said, moving closer to examine my plate, the longing clear and evident in his eyes. "I miss food."

"What was your favorite?" I asked, forgoing chopsticks in favor of a fork.

"Steak," he answered before laughing at my grimace. "Sorry, Mrs. Ex-vegetarian, but I'm an all-American guy that likes steak, fries, and soda." His face fell, even as I laughed at the image of him standing behind a grill with his family, joking and socializing with his friends. "I was... was that guy."

I took a bite and chewed slowly, watching Ryan's walls close in around him as he reflected over

145

the loss of his life. Again. There were so many times when he would refer to himself in present tense, only to catch himself and glumly make the correction to *past* tense. And it killed me every time.

"You're still that guy, I think. So you can't eat a dead animal, who cares? Everything that made you you in life is still right here." I placed my hand over my heart. "And that's all that matters."

"I'm not so sure."

"Well, I am, so don't argue with me." I pointed my fork at his face as I gave him my best stern, but reassuring smile and, eventually, he reciprocated. "Now, tell me more, Mr. Red-blooded, All-American He-man."

I ate quietly as Ryan told me stories about his life growing up. My favorite being the time he and his friends went camping at the lake and caught their grill on fire. They'd had to use an entire bag of flour to suffocate the flames, effectively ruining their dinner. And then there was the story of him and Quinn sneaking vegetables to their mother's Best-in-Show poodle at the dinner table, only to have said poodle barf on their mother's shoes over dessert.

It was so easy for me to picture Ryan in his element, laughing and causing a scene, as he spent his days surrounded by people who loved him and knew him in ways that I never would. And I had to fight to keep the green-eyed monster at bay.

As Ryan was telling me about a particularly sweet surprise he'd set up for Quinn- involving a flower arrangement and a forged letter from her favorite boy band on Valentines Day- my cell phone chirped for the third time in ten minutes and Ryan nodded at my purse.

"You can get that, you know?"

"I know," I said around a mouthful of noodles. "But it can wait."

"So can I."

I looked up and Ryan's sad smile sliced through me. Of course he could wait, but I didn't want him to. I knew that one day, Ryan would leave me. One day, he would figure out how to cross over and that would be it. I wanted to spend every second I could with this remarkable creature before he was snatched away forever.

"Just check it," he coaxed.

Rolling my eyes, I slid the phone out of my purse as he came to stand behind me.

I glanced over my shoulder. "Excuse you. What if it's personal?"

"Hey, I have zero entertainment here while you're at work. Humor me."

"Fine." I rolled my eyes before unlocking the screen and scrolling through the messages.

*Drew: We're going to Zanies. Wanna come?*

*Kayla: Drew's annoying me. Come save me. Plz!*

*Drew: Take the red line. You can be here in thirty. Bring your new man.*

The cold shift in the air told me everything I needed to know without Ryan saying a word. Whatever the reason, Ryan felt strongly about the messages left by my friends.

"Mercy," he whispered. "You have to go."

I threw my phone back on the counter. "I'd rather not."

"Why? You don't have anything better to do."

I shoveled the last bite of lo mein into my mouth before rinsing the plate in the sink. "Yes, I do."

"No, Mercy, you really don't."

My shoulders stiffened as I turned to argue, but the words dried on my tongue as I came face to face with Ryan.

"This isn't healthy," he said, struggling with the words, just as I was struggling for breath at his close proximity. "You know that. I know that."

"What isn't healthy?" I didn't want to argue. My mind was set. I didn't want to go out and I didn't want to leave Ryan behind.

"Spending so much time in this apartment by yourself." Ryan turned and strode toward the living room, where I knew he was going to sulk at his favorite spot by the window.

I followed. "Except... I'm not by myself."

"You may as well be."

My teeth chattered at the sudden drop in temperature. When Ryan was sad, or angry, or felt any twinge of strong emotional wrath tempting to take him over, it always grew cold. And Ryan was more than sad. He was miserable. I wrapped my arms around myself to fend off the cold and closed the distance between us.

"I don't want this for you, Mercy," he said, eyes downcast and hands wove through his hair in anguish. "I don't want you to be alone."

I slipped right through him, something I'd never done before. The tingly, chilling sensation moving through his presence caused lasted only a second and I fought to keep from shivering. Bracing my back against the window so he couldn't see past me, I forced him to meet my eyes as I opened myself up. He needed to see just how much I needed him, how much I wanted him, and how much I cared for him. It didn't make sense. It wasn't rational. And it one-hundred percent wasn't healthy.

But there it was.

"Then don't leave."

His blue eyes glittered, and I wondered if he could cry. Could angels cry? I had stopped using the terms 'ghost' or 'spirit' by that point, because Ryan wasn't just a soul trapped on earth. He was bound to me by something more, something neither he nor I could fully understand. He was so much more than anything I'd ever witnessed, ever felt, ever wished for. He was my angel, and I wasn't going to let him slip through my fingers if I could help it. I wasn't going to turn away from him just because of our unreasonable circumstances.

Ryan's eyes were hard, tortured, but still as compassionate as ever as he reached his hand forward to caress my cheek. My eyes fluttered closed on their own as a cold wave of comfort washed over my skin, sending pinpricks of awareness washing over my extremities.

"I watch those people down there everyday," he gestured at the window behind me, "and I'll never understand why so many of them are depressed about things in their life they can't control. Because I remember... the thing that depressed me the most was the idea that I would one day die. That I would cease to exist. That I would be blinked out of being and would only be a memory. And memories fade with time. Eventually, we all float away into the darkness."

Ryan slumped forward, but I wasn't about to let him fall into the depths of whatever he was dealing with without a lifeline. "Unless you have someone to steady you. To hold on through high tide." I tilted my head to the side, bringing my eyes inches from his so I could watch his expression as I promised what I'd never promised any soul before. "I'll be your anchor... I won't let you float away."

His blue eyes blazed, taking in my words, letting them soak into his being until it was too much for him to take. His lashes slammed together, leaving me in the dark.

My heart fell and the rational voice in my head told me to let it be, but I couldn't. I couldn't walk away.

"Don't leave," I whispered

Ryan shocked me by pulling his shoulders back and meeting my eyes. Shaking his head, as if I were a complete fool, he inched closer until his face was a mere breath from my own.

"I'm not going anywhere."

# Chapter Eleven

# Ryan

Before I knew it, my three month 'deathaversary' was upon us. Three confusing, tormenting months I'd spent as one of the dead. And yet, there were times when it wasn't confusing, it wasn't torture. As soon as that blonde angel swept through the door, all my anguish vanished like a fog burning away at sunrise.

Mercy had put her life on hold for me, and I hated myself for it. But how could I say anything when she was the only thing anchoring me to sanity? How could I even breach the topic with her, knowing that she would find some way to turn it around on herself and think I *didn't* want her company? Because she would. I knew her well enough to know that for a fact. And how could I do that to her? How could I play a part in tearing away that welcoming smile she always held for me every evening?

Easy. I couldn't.

"What's the point?"

Willa sat in the corner, braiding a pile of daisies into a crown as I waited for Mercy to return from work.

"Does there have to be a point?"

"Yes." I paced the floor, as was per usual in the hours before Mercy walked through the door. Every day I tried to talk myself into telling her to let go, to move on. And every day, as I listened to her key turn in the lock, I talked myself out of it. "There has to be a point to everything that happens. Right? Otherwise, it's just chaos."

"Chaos can be a beautiful thing," she answered absentmindedly.

"Or it can tear everything apart."

She sat her project to the side before laying back and propping her clasped hands behind her head like a pillow.

"Life is chaotic, wouldn't you say?"

"It can be." I stopped pacing and dropped to the floor beside her.

"And love? Doesn't that also carry a breeze of chaos?"

"In the beginning, maybe," I ran my hand along the carpet, feeling nothing but my cold, unyielding prison walls. "But it's also supposed to bring calm and serenity, isn't it? It's supposed to heal the broken, not tear them apart further."

"Chaos and serenity are two halves of a whole. You can't have one without the other. They touch each other. Where one ends, the other begins. Their coexistence is the foundation of everything human, everything beautiful."

"Maybe. But there still has to be a point to it all, right? What we do in life, what we say, how we treat others, who we decide to love... it all leads somewhere. It has to."

"What makes you think that love is a decision?" Willa's eyes softened. "Love isn't rational, Ryan. You can't look at someone and say, 'I'm going to love her. She's going to love me. That's how it's going to go'. It doesn't work that way. If it did, would you have chosen to love Mercy?"

Having it spelled out like that sent fireworks of pain through my chest -through my empty, non-existent, dead heart. With every day that passed, I grew to care for Mercy even more. But with every night, the truth of my feelings were laid bare as she dreamed.

"Who says I love Mercy?"

"You do," she answered certainly. "You say it with your eyes, your smile, your light... everything about you comes to life when she walks through that door."

"You're wrong," I spat, refusing to indulge in Willa's childhood fantasies of love and happily ever afters. "Nothing about me comes to life. Everything about me is laying in Oak Wood Cemetery."

"If that were true, do you think you'd still be here?" She asked. "Do you think you'd still exist if your story was over? If you don't matter, then why are you here, Ryan? What's the point? Do you think there's a deity out there who pushed you two together just for the satisfaction of watching you tear each other apart?"

"Maybe."

Willa scoffed before standing and carrying her flower crown across the room with both hands. Jumping onto the arm of the couch, she turned to me and laid the crown atop her head.

"You suffer with her, and you suffer without her. The question is, which of those sufferings hurts the most?"

Pursing my lips and staring at the floor, I refused to answer. I refused to look at Willa and spill my heart.

"Ryan. Which hurts more? The sweet ache you feel when you reach out to touch her and realize you can't? Or the endless, seething void in your being when she's outside these walls? Which is so mindlessly painful that you'd rather-"

"Suffering with her!" I yelled, putting an end to Willa's ramblings. "Happy? I would rather be with her and cause us both pain, than to suffer the sting of leaving her and losing her forever, okay? That's how selfish I am! But it doesn't matter. None of it matters because the truth is that no matter how hard I want it, there's not a damn thing I can do to change reality. And the reality is that I'm nothing." I forced myself to take a deep breath, filling lungs I no longer possessed. "And she is everything. Absolutely everything that is good and beautiful and wonderful and worth loving in life. That's the truth, Willa. But nothing can change the facts, so what's the point?"

Willa smiled like a proud teacher before nodding slowly, like I was on the brink of mastering an impossible equation. Her hazel eyes lit up as she placed one hand, then the other, over her heart.

"Love is the point, Ryan. Love is the reason."

I couldn't do it anymore. I couldn't act like this was my love story, my happily ever after, when in reality it was the most excruciating punishment ever placed on an individual's soul. Waving Willa's words away, I reclaimed my post at the window.

The city streets were blurred by the speckling of rain against the window, so I turned my face to the heavens. Watching the sky weep wasn't going to make me feel any better, but it also wouldn't make me feel any worse.

As much as I hated to admit it, Willa was right. When I was alone, my thoughts were chaotic. But when I was with Mercy, her presence wrapped me in a kind of serenity I'd never had before our worlds collided. When we were together, I was whole. And if the twinkle of affection in her eyes was any indicator, she felt the same.

Two halves of a whole. Chaos and serenity. That was love. That was what I had with a woman whose heart still beat within her chest. And for me, that was enough. What more could a dead man ask for?

But as for Mercy? Surely she had to feel as if this was the biggest joke the universe had ever played on her.

As the rain intensified, my chest constricted. It wasn't the metaphysical pain I was used to dealing with, the kind that was there but wasn't. This was a whole other feeling entirely. Something new. Puzzled by the sensation of a physical pull within my essence, I turned to Willa and the feeling doubled.

For the first time since my death, I *felt.* I could feel. And what I was feeling was shredding through my soul. The electric shock of Willa's touch was nothing compared to this. It was in my chest, my head. Everywhere. I couldn't escape the seething pain pumping through my chest, colliding in the chambers of my heart, and sparking back out in tortuous, burning embers that were seeping in and out of my pores.

"What's happening?" I choked out.

Willa flashed over to the window, looking down at the street with both a sadness and a hopefulness that sent me running when the two dreaded syllables fell from her lips.

"Mercy."

# Mercy

All day I thought of nothing but Ryan, which was ridiculous. So much time had gone by with him, and yet, not enough. I felt as if I would never get enough time. The rational part of my brain told me I shouldn't invest so much time worrying about him leaving at the drop of a hat. But rational thought was the furthest thing from my mind when I stared off into space, wondering if he was thinking about me or if he felt the same pull I felt every time I walked through the door.

The term 'crossing over' had blazed through my mind so many times the words were practically etched into my cerebral tissue. It hurt to admit it to myself, but I'd come to realize that maybe that's why Ryan was with me. Maybe it was my job to help him cross over, to help him come to whatever epiphany was required of him to be able to venture on into the next phase of his existence. And along with that realization came an idea I was nowhere near ready to accept.

Perhaps Ryan wasn't mine to keep. Maybe he was mine to help.

Soggy and dejected, I waded through puddles as the rain came down in waves, soaking through my clothing until my teeth set to chattering and my muscles trembled against the cold. It was mid-summer, but I could see my breath as the wind carried it from my mouth out into the open air, pulling it in all directions until it disappeared into the atmosphere.

*Like Ryan...*

For the millionth time, I swallowed around the lump in my throat created by the idea that Ryan could so easily be pulled away from me to be cast out into the abyss, into whatever waited for him on the other side. And I tried to convince myself of how much better that would be for him. That was how it was supposed to be, after all. Surely he wasn't meant to be trapped within the confines of a cheerless building for all eternity. He had to be destined for so much more. A soul like his deserved the most prestigious spot among the heavens- his own star in the sky where he could shine down on humanity long after the words on his tombstone eroded into dust. And yet, I was selfish enough to *not* want that.

I quickened my pace, eager to make it home to Ryan, to make sure he was still there as I did every day. Every single time I raced up the stairs, I feared I would open the door to an open apartment. I knew it was absurd, but that was my biggest fear.

Hopping across puddles and small streams breaking through the sidewalk, I made my way toward Chinatown Gate, only to be soaked in a spray of mud from a passing car.

"You have *got* to be kidding me!" I sputtered, wiping a disgusting mix of rain water and city filth from my face.

The black Mercedes continued on down the road, the driver no doubt happy, dry, and oblivious to my building agitation. After shaking myself off and wringing out my light jacket, I realized it was pointless. The rain was coming down too hard and too fast. I just needed to get home.

# Ryan

The rain tracks surfing down the window made it almost impossible for me to track her movements, but I knew it was her on the street below. Her blonde hair matted to her face as water streamed over her cheeks and she swiped at her eyes to clear her vision. She should have taken an umbrella. No, she should have taken her car.

I held my breath as I waited to see if she would glance up at the window. Could she feel my eyes on her? Did she sense when I was thinking about her?

*You're being ridiculous, Ryan. Of course not. You're a phantom. You can't possibly have any kind of real connection with that beautiful creature down there.*

Almost as if she could hear my inner musings, Mercy lifted her face and narrowed her eyes. The corners of my lips lifted up in an involuntary smile as I raised my hand to wave.

And that's when I heard it...

The rain slowed.

The world lagged.

The light dimmed.

And I broke my eyes away from Mercy's to track the sound of skidding tires.

"No."

A car, less than a block away, was careening out of control, hydroplaning on the wet asphalt. I shifted my eyes back and forth, gauging it's trajectory.

It was headed straight for Mercy.

I slammed my hands against the window and screamed as loud as my spirit would allow.

"Mercy! Mercy, move!"

I waved my arms in the direction of the car, but Mercy stood stock still, unseeing, unaware of the danger she was in. I turned to search for Willa. I needed her to do what she did before. I needed her to get me through the wall so I could get outside to Mercy.

But she was gone.

Turning back, my eyes were met with the sight of Mercy bathed in the glow of headlights.

I knew I had to do *something.* Surely I hadn't been suspended in Limbo just to watch Mercy die. That wasn't the plan, it couldn't have been. That was even more cruel than letting me fall in love with her. No. I refused to believe that. I was supposed to protect her. I had to. I just needed to be stronger than whatever held me prisoner.

Slamming my eyes shut, I pressed my hands against the cold glass, focusing everything- my energy, my being, my soul, my *heart*- on being outside in the rain with Mercy. I prayed to God to let

161

me go to her, to let me save her. I bargained. I screamed. I pleaded. I pushed so hard until...

I was falling.

The wind rushed through my hair for three stories, slowly at first, and then rapidly as time regained it's normal pace. The second my body made contact with the pavement, I was up and running as the screech of tires and neglected brake pads filled the air. My feet found purchase on the wet asphalt and I took off down the street, pushing myself for all I was worth.

The black Mercedes was moving too fast. Getting closer to Mercy. But I wasn't letting that happen. I sailed through the rain- pushing, praying, and ignoring everything else until I was where I needed to be. Where I was meant to be.

With Mercy...

My beautiful, blonde angel looked up with wide, fearful eyes as I concentrated every ounce of awareness, every feeling of hope, and every drop of *love* I had in my soul on saving her.

Opening my arms wide, I reached for her and, ever so gracefully, we collided with a warmth and softness that only the living can possess as I fought to pull her out of the way.

Then everything began to blur.

A blinding blast of white flooded my vision as my arms grew heavy and weak, causing me to let go of Mercy. "No! Mercy, no!" I shook my head, fighting to open my eyes against the blinding light as I scrambled for her, reaching out in hopes of finding her and anchoring her against me, body to body. Soul to soul.

But my hands came back empty as I listened to the woman I loved say my name one last time.

"Ryan!"

And then she was gone.

The rain, the street, the car- everything disappeared.

No matter how hard I tried to hold onto her, to stay behind for her, I couldn't fight the force latching onto my soul and dragging me away as I kicked, screamed, and fought like hell to reclaim Mercy.

"No!" I cried as she was stripped away from me. "I won't leave her! I'm going back! I'm not leaving!"

"I'm sorry, Ryan."

I shielded my eyes against the hot glare as I searched for Willa's face.

"Right here, sweetie."

I blinked and narrowed my eyes, finally zoning in on her tiny, retreating form across the endless void placed at my feet. She was so far away. I couldn't reach her any more than I could reach Mercy. I was losing Willa as well.

As my feet left the ground and I was lifted away from everything I didn't want to leave, I caught a glimpse of Willa's face. To my surprise, she was smiling.

"Thank you."

"What do you mean?" I demanded. "Thank you for what? For what, Willa?"

But the answer never came.

She was gone.

I was leaving.

And I would never see Mercy again.

They say the dead can't feel pain.

They're wrong.

What I felt was a searing-hot, breath-stealing, heart-crushing, soul-deep misery I couldn't escape. A pain I knew I was going to be saddled with for all eternity.

# Chapter Twelve

## Mercy

*Ryan?*
*Are you there?*
*Where am I?*
The shrill beeping of monitors jarred me awake. Lifting my head off the pillow, I looked around at the dark, empty room. From the dimmed florescent bulbs set into the low ceiling to the scuffed white tiles making up the floor- everything looked different. Everything was off, like the world wasn't spinning quite like it should have been.

And then it all came crashing back.

The rain.

The squealing.

The car.

And then...

"Ryan?"

Silence greeted me with a sneer as I lifted up in bed and carefully dropped my legs off the side. After waiting to see if my body could withstand being upright, I set off in search of answers.

What happened? Where was I? Had someone called my family? When could I go home? I had to go home. I had to see Ryan. I had a million questions bubbling up inside of me that I needed answered. And only he could answer them. I needed to go.

Blowing through a closed curtain, I turned to find a morose looking brunette sitting behind a tall receptionist desk. I approached her with caution, not knowing if I was allowed out of bed, let alone out of my room.

"Excuse me? Is my family here by any chance?"

She made a small notation in a chart, but didn't answer my question. She didn't even acknowledge that I'd spoken.

"Mercy. Hunter. That's my name. Is my family here yet?"

Nothing. Not a shake of a head, not a finger held up to silence me, nothing.

*Rude...*

"Hello? I'm talking to you." I waved my hand in front of her face, but aside from a bored sigh, she went on ignoring me.

"Fine," I huffed before taking off in search of the waiting room.

I circled around the floor twice, never finding anything resembling a waiting room. Feeling more lost by the second, I ventured down the stairwell until I reached the ground floor. My socks padded silently

166

across the sterilized concrete as I neared the emergency room doors. They opened and closed automatically as nurses, doctors, and staff rushed from place to place. The seats in the lobby were all vacant, but a lone man stood at a pay phone just inside the doors. His shoulders shook as he sobbed garbled words into the receiver, and something about his posture struck a chord.

"Lyric?" I sped toward him, holding my arms out to my sides so I wouldn't slip on the smooth floor. "What's the matter? I'm right here, bub. Everything's fine. Look! See? I'm okay."

As I reached out for him, he slammed the receiver down, cursed, and flew toward the door.

"Lyric, wait!" I called after him.

I tried to run, tried to tell him that everything was okay, but I couldn't. A dizzy spell grabbed hold of my skull and sunk its fingers deep into my brain, making me cry out in pain. Or was it pain? No. Not pain, exactly. Just pressure.

I could barely keep my feet under me as it felt like my spine was breaking away. Like every vertebrae was a puzzle piece falling to the floor. I shouldn't have gotten out of bed. That was a mistake. Something was definitely wrong and I needed to find my way back to my room.

Carefully, I climbed the stairs, only to curse myself as I showed up at my previous floor and realized there was an elevator bay mere feet from the same door leading to the stairs.

*Pat on the back for you, Mercy. Way to be an idiot.*

Retracing my steps, I shuffled back toward my

room. The doors and curtains weren't numbered, so I walked and walked in search of the rude brunette and an empty bed.

But there were no empty beds. Every corner I turned confused me further. As nurses sped past, I tried to grab their attention, I tried to ask for help, but my voice went on unheard.

Panic set in as I realized no one would even spare me a glance.

Threading my fingers through my hair in frustration, I whirled around and around in search of anything familiar, anyone who looked like they could help me. But the hallway had emptied, and I was alone. My knees gave out and I found myself sitting on the tile floor with my face buried in my hands, seconds away from a complete emotional breakdown.

"Are you okay?"

The soft soprano voice halted my tears and I looked up through my curtain of hair to see a little girl perched on the corner of the receptionist's desk. Her long brown hair was braided in pig tails and she offered me a kind smile as she played with the stethoscope draped around her neck.

"Yeah," I sniffed. "I'm fine. Just a little lost."

"No you're not," she said confidently. "You're exactly where you're supposed to be."

The tiny girl hopped off the desk with all the grace of a seasoned ballerina before strolling over to meet me, swinging the stethoscope in circles as she walked.

"Don't worry, Mercy. It gets better. I promise."

"Who- what? Do I know you?" I asked. "Have we met before?"

She nodded. "We've met before and we'll meet again."

And then, she set off skipping down the hall.

"Wait!" I yelled after the child, desperate for her to stay. "Where are you going?"

She smiled over her shoulder as her pig tails bounced with each silent step. "I have to go! We're late!"

Her giggling laughter faded as I pulled my knees to my chest and watched her disappear around the corner. Everything dimmed in her absence. Everything quieted. Pressing my forehead to my knees, I clenched my jaw to keep from crying. I couldn't cry. I had to figure out what was going on.

And then I heard them.

Footsteps.

Fast, quick, and determined.

I don't know how, but I was certain those footsteps were for me. Whoever was running was searching for me. The echoed slapping of bare feet and desperation compelled me to stand and as I turned, I was met with the only sight I would have welcomed at that point.

Blue eyes crashed into blue eyes.

"There you are!"

Without a trace of hesitation, I ran to him. Smiling, I barely stopped in time to keep from falling through him.

"You're here! I can't believe you're really here. I don't even know how that happened. How'd you leave? That was- I can't even begin to tell you how thankful I am. I just- I'm so happy to see you."

My voice caught as I took in the sad eyes

169

bearing down on me. Ryan stared, looking so dejected that all I wanted to do was hug him until all the negative emotion drained from his body and all that was left was Mercy-inspired bliss.

But I couldn't. I knew better.

"What's wrong?"

Ryan's blue eyes trailed up and down my body, taking me all in, before struggling to fight back a sob. And just as before, as I was staring down the grill of a Mercedes, my breath was stolen as Ryan wrapped his arms around my shoulders and buried his face in my hair. Instinct told me to wrap my arms around his waist and... I froze.

"Ryan? I can feel you." I pulled away as a sob broke through my chest. I touched his arms, his shoulders, his face, his hair. "I can feel you! Oh my God!"

It felt so good to touch him that I completely disregarded the tortured mask weighing down his face. I felt his muscles beneath his t-shirt, his collarbone, the soft firmness of his abdominal muscles, the subtle curve of his neck...

"Mercy." He grabbed my hands and pulled them to his chest. "Stop."

"I don't understand. This is amazing!"

He stepped away, trying to distance himself so I would listen, but I wasn't letting him get far. I had to do it. Had to. There wasn't a single reason not to. Erupting in a triumphant giggle, I threw my arms around his neck and pulled his body into mine, quieting both of us as I pressed my lips to his.

It was nothing like I'd imagined. His lips felt... warm. Warm and soft and perfect against my own. His

170

firm arms wound around my waist and his solid chest collided with mine as he easily held my weight against his.

*Pure perfection. Complete undiluted bliss.*

"Wow" I breathed as I pulled away in a frazzled daze. "How are you doing this? I can feel that, Ryan. I can feel everything."

Looking up, I fell silent. Ryan wasn't smiling. He wasn't laughing. He wasn't celebrating. Instead, he looked heart-stoppingly broken.

"What's wrong?"

With a stuttered breath, he dropped his forehead to mine and closed his eyes. "Everything's wrong, Mercy. Everything in this whole damn world is wrong."

"What do you mean?" I shook my head, refusing to let him ruin the perfection of the moment. "What are you talking about?"

The dinging of the elevator doors opening caught both our attentions and I moved to pull us out of the way, but a familiar head of frizzy, wild hair caught my eye.

There were my parents, working their way through the elevator doors. And I'd never been so happy to see them in all my life.

"Mom! Dad!"

My heart somersaulted in my chest as I left Ryan's side and rushed across the hall. Weaving in and out of the crowd, I squealed with pure joy as I jumped up to embrace my father...

Only to end up alone in the elevator.

"Dad?"

Confused, I spun around and watched my

parents retreat down the corridor. Both sobbing, both holding soaked tissues to their faces.

"Mom! Dad! Where are you going? Stop!"

"Mercy." Ryan arrived at my side, pulling me back into his body, but I stiffened. My arms braced themselves against his chest and pushed.

"No. Let me go." I wrestled my way out of his grip and turned to follow my parents. "Mom! Come back. Mom! It's me! Why aren't you listening to me?"

"Mercy, please." Ryan caught my arm and whirled me back around to face him.

"Why won't they stop?" I sobbed. "It's like they can't even hear-"

Ryan pulled me into his arms. His warm, comforting arms. Arms I could feel beneath my own.

Warm arms. Ryan was warm.

Or I was cold.

"No," I gasped. "No, tha- that's impossible!" I pushed away, scrambling to catch myself as he hung on, both of us trying to keep me from falling to the ground.

"Mercy, just listen to me, please."

"No! This isn't right. Something- something's wrong. I'm here. I'm right here! I-I can see and hear and feel and..." I stuttered as I tore my fingers through my hair. Spinning, I turned to find my parents gone and the hall emptied of people once again. It was just me and Ryan. "But- but you were there. You pulled me out of the way. You saved me! You did, I felt it. I just- I... I am not dead! Ryan, you came and you saved me and I'm going to be fine. This is just-"

"You're not going to be fine!" Ryan screamed as he grabbed my shoulders and shook. "I didn't save you, Mercy! I tried. I swear to God, I tried, but I couldn't. I couldn't save you!"

"That's not true." I shook my head, refusing to believe, refusing to accept that I was gone. I couldn't be. I felt so alive, more so than I'd felt in months, hell, *years* even.

"I was supposed to protect you," Ryan's voice cracked. "But I couldn't."

He looked just as lost as I felt, and I didn't even know where to begin. I didn't know how to fight off the urge to slam my fists into the ground over and over until someone told me that there had been a mistake. I fought to keep from running through the halls, screaming, thrashing, tearing at my hair until every doctor in the hospital acknowledged my cries and stepped in to help me.

"I'm sorry, Mercy. I would give anything, and I do mean *anything*, to change this. I'd sell my soul to the devil right now if it meant that you could keep on breathing."

"You- you didn't save me?" I squeaked.

"No, love," he pulled me back into his arms and I went willingly. "I didn't."

Ryan rocked me, back and forth, until the confusion, the absence of pain, the injustice of it all just fell away.

Looking up into eyes as blue as the sea and as broken as a capsized ship, Ryan gazed down at me, speaking millions of promises with just one look.

"Why?" Holding his face in my hands, I pulled his forehead to mine, silently asking for life, for breath, for a million other things he couldn't give me. "I don't want to die."

"I know." He softly kissed my temple, sending a warmth and comfort across my skin that I'd prayed for every day for months while still alive. "I don't want that either."

Quietly, something nagged at the back of my mind. A memory. It tugged on my ear, forcing me to acknowledge it's presence.

"You left?"

"I did," Ryan answered somberly.

"But you're here."

"Because I found my way back," he smiled. "I fought."

"Fought what? Who? That doesn't make any sense."

Ryan tucked a strand of hair behind my ear before moving both hands to caress my cheek. "No, it doesn't, but I'm not questioning it. I'm just thanking God for giving me a second chance."

Death wasn't a second chance. Death was the end, right? At least, that's what I'd always assumed. "Second chance to do what?"

Ryan wrapped me in his arms and held on for dear life. "To save you."

"I don't understand," I whispered against the warmth of his neck.

"Do you honestly believe there's a reason for everything?"

I pulled away. Of course he knew that, I'd told him that once before. "Yes, but-"

"I failed, Mercy, but maybe that's not the point. Because my death, no matter how much I try to deny it, was my salvation. I was an empty human being. Yes, there were people I cared for and things I

174

was passionate about, but I was never able to appreciate anything until I was sent to you."

"Sent to me?" My voice sounded tiny, broken.

"I've never felt more alive, more important, than I was with you. You made me feel like I mattered." He placed my palm above his heart. "And I wanted the same for you."

He wasn't making any sense. I mattered. So?

"So, maybe there's something more," he pressed on. "Maybe we're just the seeds. And maybe fate is the water and divinity is the sun."

"And the flowers?" The words fell from my mouth even though I didn't understand them.

"I'm not sure yet. But do you feel that?" He pressed my hand harder into his chest, until my palm was met with the sweet beating of the heart I'd fallen so in love with.

"Yes... I feel it."

Ryan pulled me close and I closed my eyes as I laid my ear against his torso, listening to the sound I'd wanted so badly to fall asleep to every night.

*Thump-thump, thump-thump, thump-thump, thump-...........*

"Ryan?"

I pulled away in shock, only to be greeted by a vast void of nothingness. Nothing but white. Nothing but my earthly body, empty space, and...

"Hold on tight."

Ryan took my hands in his and positioned my arms around his waist before cocooning me in his protective embrace.

"What's happening?" I mumbled against his chest, shaking as I tried to process what was coming to life around us. "I'm scared."

"Me too. Just don't let go, okay? Promise me you won't let go."

As the light grew even more magnificent, our souls trembled and I clenched my eyes shut- knowing that whatever was happening, I was with Ryan and nothing- not God or the Devil himself- could tear us apart.

"I promise."

*Reach for me*
*Don't let go*
*I'll catch up*
*Just take it slow.*

*Let me in*
*Don't be afraid*
*What we lost*
*Is worth the trade.*

*Just give up*
*We paid the price*
*It'll all be worth*
*Our sacrifice*
*When we're together...*

# Chapter Thirteen

## Lyric

*Dead?*
*No.*
*Impossible.*

It had been days since we'd received the call, but I still refused to believe, refused to accept that Mercy was gone. It still seemed completely surreal. Like, at any moment, the landlord was going to call back and say, "Sorry! She's not really dead. My bad!" But I knew that wasn't going to happen. After receiving the initial call from Alice Whitlock, more calls had poured in from friends all over the continental U.S. who had heard of Mercy's passing. News like that traveled fast among our people.

I spent the better part of three hours on the

phone, listening to people who knew our family offer their condolences. And the entire time I was one-hundred percent numb. It wasn't real. Couldn't be. How could a world without Mercy, without my beautiful baby sister, exist? It couldn't. It didn't seem plausible.

Eventually, the numbness wore off, as I knew it would, and I realized how naive my line of thinking had been. She *was* gone. I could feel it in my bones, in my heart. In my soul. She was really, truly, gone forever. I'd never get to ruffle her hair again, or tease her about being the black sheep. I'd never get to watch her walk down the aisle at her wedding or be there when she gave birth to my niece or nephew. All those possibilities and more- gone. Vanished.

Aside from naivety, a whole other terror greeted me as the numbing sensation receded: Pain. Incredible, suffocating pain like nothing I'd felt before. I'd never suffered a loss, especially of someone so close to my heart, and it was like taking the most brutal beating of my life. In all honesty, getting beat would have been better. Maybe I could have gotten a few hits in myself to whoever was doing the beating. Normally, I was a pacifist and the thought of violence sickened me. But not that day. Not when I got the call that my sister had been taken. Right then, I wanted to hurt someone. I wanted to tear them down to my level and hold them by the throat. I wanted to ask them if they could feel what I was feeling, if it would ever go away, or if, maybe, they could put me out of my misery.

"Lyric, sweetie?"

My mother's tearful words seemed to swim

through the air, against the current, fighting to be heard over the rest of the world. I looked up to find her face crumpled, her posture bleak, and her eyes void of any and all light. She looked like the embodiment of what I was feeling.

"Watcha need, mama?" I asked softly.

"Can you..." She covered her eyes with the palm of her hand as her bottom lip trembled. "Can you please go find your father?"

"Where'd he go? I thought he was with you?"

She forced her shoulders back as she wiped at her eyes, trying ever so gracefully to keep it together for the sake of the family. But she didn't have to do that. She didn't have to be strong. No one did. We were all adults- no one had to be taken care of. Mercy had been the baby. Maybe it wasn't time to be strong, maybe it was time to fall apart.

But I couldn't tell her that. If she wanted to try and be strong, to put on a front, I'd let her. Whatever she needed, however she needed to feel- I wasn't going to stop her.

"He left. Just got up and walked out. I don't know where he went and he wouldn't talk to me so-"

When her voice started wavering again, I laid what I hoped was a reassuring hand on her back as she fought to compose herself. "I'll find him. Just sit here. Don't answer the phone if you don't feel like it, okay? I'll be right back."

I kissed the top of my mother's head and made my way out the front door of a house that wasn't ours. There was only one phone in our neighborhood and it was three houses down from where my parents called home. Jogging the short distance, I let my eyes roam

180

up and down the street, looking for some sign of my father.

It wasn't like him to just disappear. He was the backbone of our family. When we all fell short, he was there to pick us up, dust us off, and reassure us that there was always tomorrow. He'd say, "The sun will set. Then it will rise. You'll figure it out with fresh new eyes." That hadn't made much sense to me growing up, but now, as a grown man, it was my mantra.

With every day that passed, I made it a point to see new things, new places, new people. Even though I'd been working as a photographer for years, I still wasn't sure if that's what I wanted to do. Most people dream about different career paths- I know Mercy did, but not me. Nothing ever seemed to draw me in. There wasn't one single thing on earth I looked at and said, "Yes. I was meant for that." So, I roamed town to town, state to state, searching the country for that 'thing', that calling that reached out and grabbed me.

Mercy had found that. I'd felt it during my visit. But it wasn't her job that had grounded her, or even her apartment, or that damn cell phone she was so set on having... It was something else. It could have been the city, that was possible. Or it could have been her new friends, I have no idea, I didn't stay long enough to find out. But there had definitely been something that reached out for her, that spoke to her in ways nothing else had. Because for the first time in our entire life, she seemed to be at peace. So much more at peace than I'd ever be again, I knew that much.

Reaching the front porch of my parents' house,

I hurdled over all three stairs and bounced straight through the open door, still jogging, still searching for my father.

"Dad?" I sailed through the living room, around the kitchen, pushed open every bathroom and bedroom door, and found nothing. "Dad, where are you?"

There was one place left in the house, but the thought of him being down in the dark basement during a time like this made me queasy. That room sucked the life out of me on my best days, so I wasn't sure that venturing below ground- especially when I was flooded with mental images of Mercy being lowered down in a casket- was something I was able to do.

Turning toward the back of the house, I found the basement door cracked. Heaving out a sigh and sending up a silent prayer to the gods, I ventured down the stairs, one at a time, until the cool darkness enveloped me.

"Dad?" I felt along the walls- walls my father had built over the bare dirt and cement that had been in place when Mercy claimed it as her room. "Dad, are you down here?"

My hand fumbled over the light switch and after an almost inaudible click, the room flooded with light.

There was my father. Laying on Mercy's old bed. Weeping.

"Dad?" There was no point in asking if he was alright. Obviously, he wasn't. None of us were. But I didn't know what else to say. I had no words of consolation. I had no wisdom or philosophy that could ease the pain that was clearly ripping my father to pieces. So, I didn't say anything. I simply lowered myself to the tile floor and gripped his hand in mine with a fierceness I hoped communicated that I was there for him, that I wasn't going anywhere, and that I was hurting just as much as he was over the loss of the one soul who had always burned brightest in our family.

"She's gone," he sobbed quietly. "My Mercy is gone."

# Quinn

"Hello?"

I answered the phone with the phoniest, most upbeat voice I could muster. I had to. Otherwise, the pity that rang out from the other end of the line would crush me.

"Yes, may I speak with Mrs. Callahan?"

"This is she."

"Quinn, is it?" The disembodied voice asked with pity that I hadn't even deserved.

"Yes, may I ask who's speaking?"

"This is Mark, from Bradford Monuments."

I closed my eyes and carefully breathed through my nose, trying to keep my composure. This was the call I had been waiting for. The last step in putting Ryan to rest was finally here.

"It's being delivered, Mrs. Callahan. Should be in place by the end of the week."

Carefully clearing my throat, I asked, "Have you contacted my parents?"

"No, ma'am, but not for lack of trying. I called

but there was never any answer. But your name was also listed on the paperwork, so..."

"Of course, yes." I wasn't sure what to say. I'd never dealt with something like this before and I wasn't sure what the proper etiquette would be. "Well, thank you, sir. My family appreciates everything you've done. I guess I'll, uh, I'll be out to see it this weekend."

"Pleasure was all mine, ma'am. I'm sorry for your loss."

Before my voice had a chance to break, I ended the call and released the breath I hadn't realized I'd been holding. This was it. It was really happening. My final goodbye.

It had been over three months since Ryan's death, but I was still finding it hard to put one foot in front of the other. It hurt. God, did it hurt. And the worst part was that I *knew.* No one else, not even the coroner, *knew* the moment he had died. But I did. I knew he had died in the middle of the night. There had only been one moment of heightened discomfort as he woke, one moment of searing pain, and then he was called home.

I knew all of that, because I'd been awake. I'd been sitting up in bed, reading to myself after a long day of work when *SNAP.* My chest seized and it felt as if whatever string had been keeping me from floating away from the world had been cut. It felt like gravity itself no longer had an effect on me and I was floating away, trying my hardest to stay tethered to the Earth.

But, I hadn't moved. I was still in my bed, in my room, in my cozy apartment. But as soon as my chest filled with dread, as soon as a dark emptiness filled every single vein in my body... I knew. I knew something had happened. And I'd been right.

Shaking my head in an attempt to rid myself of the memories of that horrible night, I dialed my parents' number and tapped my foot nervously as I waited for someone to pick up.

"Callahan residence."

My mother's voice was stern, controlled, as it always had been. She wasn't a hard or unfeeling woman, but one might think that just from having a brief conversation with her.

I loved my parents, but they had made Ryan's death hell on me. They didn't do it consciously, but still, I had to keep myself at a distance if I ever wanted to deal with them. If I didn't, their words would break me all over again.

"Mom, it's Quinn."

"Hello, sweetie. How've you been?"

The words were normal enough for an exchange between mother and daughter, but her tone was flat, empty- as if she were talking to a telemarketer or someone who had the wrong number.

"I just-" I swallowed around the knot in my throat, still finding it hard to talk about Ryan, even to the woman who gave birth to him. "I just wanted to let you know that the monument place called and they're having Ryan's headstone delivered this week."

"Well, it's about time."

That seemed like a cruel thing to say in light of the topic, but judging by the quiver in her voice, it was just her way of coping. But even if that was the case, I was her daughter. She didn't have to put on a front for me.

"Well, mother, I would assume that carving words into a giant slab of granite would be a rather time consuming ordeal, wouldn't you?"

My mother sighed and the sound made the muscle in my jaw tick. I hated that sound. I'd heard it one too many times growing up when Ryan and I had interrupted her while she was working to ask for something that 'could have waited'. I clenched my teeth as I reminded myself that she was not an unloving mother, she was just... difficult.

"Yes, I suppose you're right. Are you going out to see it?"

My jaw came unhinged and nearly hit the floor. Was she serious?

"Of course I'm going to see it! Aren't you?"

Another sigh.

"I just don't think your father and I are ready for that, Quinn."

Unbelievable. She wasn't even going to go see her son's headstone?

I covered my eyes in hope of escaping the red I was seeing. It didn't help. It was still there.

I snapped.

"And do you think *I'm* ready for that? Do you think that *I* was ready for my brother to be put into the ground forever? Do you think *I'm* any more capable of dealing with this than you two? Because if that's what you think, you're wrong. He wasn't just taken from you, he was taken from all of us. He was taken from me." My voice cracked and I held my breath to contain the sob threatening to shatter it's way through my chest. "You don't understand," I whispered once I

187

regained the ability to speak. "You'll never understand. I realize you lost a son, but you don't seem to realize that I lost half of myself."

A muffled sniffle from my mother told me I'd crossed the line. I couldn't continue this conversation. Not without losing it completely.

"I've gotta go, mother. I'll see you... whenever I see you."

With shaking hands and tears blurring my vision, I ended the call and dropped my phone to the floor.

# Chapter Fourteen

# Lyric

Standing at the foot of my sister's grave, watching as her coffin slowly made the descent into darkness, I realized just how unfair life was turning out to be. From my travels, I'd met all kinds of people, both good and bad. And those bad people- all the crooks, lowlifes, and flat out dangerous people? They were all still breathing. They were living and laughing while my sister- the most pure, intelligent, and sweetest person I'd ever had the honor to love- was dead.

It wasn't fair. It wasn't right. It just... *was.*

Before the quiet machine lowering Mercy's body into the ground had finished it's job, I bolted. I couldn't stay there and watch my parents and their close friends toss dirt onto my little sister's casket. I couldn't. I had been one hell of a rock during the last few days, but there was only so much pain I could withstand before breaking. And I was quickly nearing that point.

I couldn't get a grip on my overwhelming panic as the reality of my sister heading to her final resting place sank it's way into my heart. With every inch she ventured deeper, I felt as if I was being pulled in after her. If my parents wanted to stay til the very end, that was fine. But not me. I couldn't stay a single second longer.

Jogging from the grave site, I made my way to one of the many roads slicing through Oak Wood Cemetery and slowed to a walk. Just putting that much distance between me and the grim scene made me feel lighter, like I could breathe again, even though the cold bite to the September air was burning my throat with every deep breath.

It would figure that I'd have to drive to Chicago in the middle of the city's first freak snow storm of the year. From my understanding, snow wasn't due there until November, but I guess timing doesn't matter to whatever deity throws flakes from the sky. Just as timing didn't matter to whoever decided it was time to end a young woman's life.

The light dusting of snow made everything seem so beautiful, and yet, more dismal at the same time. Death was the only finality I understood. I believed whole-heartedly that there was an afterlife- a beautiful place you ventured to after death, but right then, right there, standing in the middle of so many lost loved ones... I just couldn't see it. Maybe it was selfish, but someone had been ripped out of my life and I couldn't focus on where their soul had gone. All

I knew was the pain. The loss. The all-encompassing despair.

Letting the tears fall, I walked along the deserted road. I walked and walked until I wasn't sure which way to turn. I didn't remember how many lefts or how many rights I'd taken- and it was a big cemetery- but I didn't care. My heart, my soul, my spirit- they were all lost. Might as well add 'physical being' to the list.

As I crested a hill, my breath heaving out in white puffs, something stopped me. A sound. It was close enough to hear, but not close enough to distinguish. Turning in a tight circle, I narrowed my eyes in search of the source.

There, only two rows down, was a woman. She looked thin, even through her thick coat, and I could tell she was shaking. Her long brown hair fell in front of her eyes and she kept sweeping it out of her face. Still, strands of it stuck to the tear-trails making their way through her makeup.

When the wind died down and she no longer had to fight off her hair, her arms fell limp at her sides and I was thrown back to another place, another time, when someone else had dropped their shoulders in defeat and another member of the Hunter clan was there to offer a drop of reassurance in such a dark and desperate time...

---------------------------------------------

*Six year old Mercy pulled me down the alley behind our house, intent on making me help her carry handfuls of wild daisies she'd found growing along*

191

*the side of the street. Being mid-summer in Arizona, I*
*was already hot and wanted to go home and sit*
*beneath the ceiling fan, but she was persistent.*

   *"C'mon, Lyric! They're right over here!" She*
*dropped to her knees in the gravel and began*
*gathering as many as her tiny arms could carry.*
*"Mommy will love these!"*

   *As soon as both our arms were full and I*
*begrudgingly started to follow her back to the house,*
*she stopped cold. Not watching where I was going, I*
*almost plowed right over her.*

   *"Mercy, jeez! What are you doing?"*

   *"Look."*

   *Irritated and sweaty, I followed her gaze until*
*it landed on the scene she was witnessing.*

   *A father and son in their back yard, heads*
*hung low and smiles non-existent, as they buried their*
*family dog. As the father dug the shovel into the dirt,*
*emptying out a spot for their beloved pet to rest, the*
*son stood trembling- arms at his sides, hands*
*clenched into fists- determined to keep it all in.*

   *"Gimme those."*

   *I turned to find Mercy pushing all of her haul*
*into one arm and gesturing for my own armful.*

   *"Why?"*

   *"Just give 'em!" She demanded as she*
*grabbed small handfuls, one at a time, until she had*
*so many flowers in her face she could barely see.*

   *Without another word, Mercy walked over to*
*the duo, placed the flowers at the foot of the crude*
*grave, and stepped back before reaching for the boy's*
*hand.*

   *The father, taken aback by the compassion*

192

*given freely from a small hippie child, stared wide-eyed as his son took one deep, bracing breath before letting out a resigned sigh. Then, as if that wasn't the strangest thing he'd ever witnessed, went right back to digging.*

*Mercy and the boy stood quietly, still holding hands. Two complete strangers brought together by the culmination of grief and the urge to help those who were finding it difficult to cope. It was, in a word, breathtaking.*

*When Mercy returned, I asked her why she'd done it. My question wasn't negative or derogatory- I was just curious as to her reasoning. I thought maybe it was because she felt connected to the boy, maybe she knew him from school, maybe she'd played with the dog before, or maybe just because she felt sad for him. But the words out of her six year old mouth were the last I expected.*

*"Because he needed me to."*

---------------------------------------

That was it. Seeing the woman standing in front of her loved one's grave with tears washing away her perfect makeup, I felt the same.

It was clear she needed comfort. She needed solace. She needed *someone.*

Maybe she needed me.

# Quinn

Ryan and I shared that mysterious 'twin vibe' when we were younger, but somehow, as we grew, it slowly dimmed. It was still there, just quietly tip-toeing in the background instead of screaming for attention as it had during our childhood. But standing there, at the foot of my twin brother's grave, I felt like that connection was somehow restored. I felt... peaceful. Calm. Serene. For the first time since his death, I actually felt like everything was going to be okay.

"Hey, bub." I wiped tears from my face as a half-sob, half-laugh tore from my throat. "The stone is beautiful, don't you think? I love it. I think you would too. Mom tried picking out this horribly gaudy one with a stone angel with its wings spread big and wide." I held my hands out, pantomiming the angel's pose. "But I told her that was way too much. You wouldn't have wanted that, would you? So, I fought for this one. And I hope I did okay."

The wind picked up, sending my hair flying

around my face, and I fought to keep it out of my eyes.

"It figures, I finally get all dressed up and out of the house, and my hair and makeup gets ruined." I chuckled as I wiped at my eyes. "Bet you'd get a kick out of that, huh? You always did complain about all the 'girly stuff' I liked. You used to hate it when mom made us get all dolled up for family photos. She used to squeeze us so close together my makeup would rub off on your face. Or your clothes. Remember that time, freshman year, when we used our lunch break to meet mom and dad at the photographers? And you went back to school and your girlfriend, oh, what was her name?... Jenny! She got so mad because my foundation smudged your collar. She was so sure you were cheating on her." I laughed, remembering how angry he'd been after she dumped him, but quickly sobered at the thought of how I'd never again be in a family picture with my better half. "But, you know, I'd give anything to have you back. I'd let Hell swallow me up right now if it meant you got to live a little while longer."

More tears stung my eyes as the wind picked up, sending snow skittering across my boots as I struggled to breathe.

"I don't think he'd want that."

My eyes snapped up to find an odd looking man walking along the gravel path just to my right. His long dark hair and shadowed eyes were starkly contrasted against the layer of snow blanketing everything around us, but there was something attractive about the dark cloud surrounding his demeanor. Attractive... or familiar. I wasn't sure. But

195

aside from looking different in the green vintage coat he wore over a faded t-shirt and layers of necklaces, and aside from the fact that he seemed to be working through the same kind of grief I was at that moment- there was something else about his presence.

A draw. Spiritual -not physical- attraction.

The hairs on the back of my neck stood on end and the pull I felt towards him was instantaneous and so powerful I drew in a breath. Never before had I felt something like that. I was a logical woman. Things like that didn't happen to me. And if they did, I usually ignored them. But I couldn't ignore the man standing in front of me, looking so sallow and broken my feet took a step in his direction all on their own.

"What did you say?" I asked breathlessly.

"I said he wouldn't want that. For Hell to swallow you so he could come back. I don't know who he is -or was- but no one would want that for someone they loved. No one."

At the word 'loved', his voice broke and he moved his eyes away, turning to hide the grief painted ever so vividly across his dark eyes. It may not have been the most logical, or sane, thing to do, but I took a step toward him. Then another. And another.

In a matter of seconds, I was standing in front of him, taking him in, eying him curiously as the fog of our breaths mingled between our bodies.

"Quinn Callahan." My hand shot out in greeting, and he looked down at it like he'd never been offered a handshake before. One eyebrow quirked up, before a slow smile spread across his handsome face.

After a moment, his large, warm palm pressed

196

into mine and his firm grip threw a shudder down my body. Luckily, with the wind and snow, I was able to brush it off as a shiver due to the temperature.

"Quinn Callahan," he repeated. "That's an interesting name. Little weird, actually."

Surprised by this strangers audacity, I pulled my hand back slowly and returned it to my pocket. "Oh, really? I happen to like it actually. What kind of normal, boring name were you graced with, if you don't mind me asking?"

His eyes sparkled with mischief as he pulled his shoulders back in confidence and said, "Lyric Hunter."

A laugh exploded from my lips. I couldn't help it. 'Quinn Callahan' had nothing on 'Lyric Hunter' in the weird department.

"MY name is weird? You're joking, right?"

"No." He shook his head in a show of seriousness, even as he fought to contain a smile. "Lyric Moon-Breeze Hunter is as normal as names get."

Another laugh rolled through my chest. "Where in the world did you come up with *that*?" I asked, thinking that had to be the most ludicrous made-up name I'd ever heard.

"Creative parents."

"Uh huh, right. No parents on earth would ever name their child something so-"

The dark eyed stranger held up a finger, silencing me as he reached into his back pocket and withdrew his wallet, never once breaking eye contact.

Flipping open the wallet in his hand, he held it up, eye level, so I could read the name on his license.

197

And my eyes flew wide.

"Oh my gosh, I'm so sorry. I didn't mean to make fun of your name. I honestly thought you were joking. I swear, I don't normally make fun of people's, well... anything. I just thought it was so out there that- no, I don't mean 'out there'. I just meant..." I realized I was rambling and pumped the brakes. "I'm sorry. What I meant was, I'm sorry."

"I'm thoroughly offended!" He said, even though his eyes were alight with glee and his smile said he wasn't offended at all. "I think you should make it up to me."

Tilting my head to the side and narrowing my eyes, I took in the stranger with the funny name. The draw was still there, amplified even, up close.

"And how would I go about doing that?" I asked cautiously.

"Well..." He tilted his own head to the side, mirroring my action. "You could start by letting me buy you a drink."

The irony was not lost on me. I didn't go to the cemetery to smile, and I sure as hell didn't go there to meet men. But there we were. Two broken, grieving souls, standing in the middle of acres of lost loves.

Virtually every voice in my head was screaming for me to run away. He wasn't the kind of man I usually spent time with. He was different. Unconventional. Unruly. And a million other 'un' words I couldn't even think of at the moment. The voices told me to say, 'thanks, but no thanks' and walk away. Other voices told me not to answer at all, and instead change the subject. But there was one voice, one soft, deep, kind voice in the back of my head that was whispering two words. Two very distinct words.

*Say yes.*

I painfully realized that the voice sounded too much like the man laying peacefully six feet beneath the snow covered earth. The man who always told me to throw my inhibitions to the wind and start to live, even though he never once took his own advice. He had died in his apartment, completely alone, and would never have the chance to love someone, to throw his own inhibitions to the wind and drive through life with all the force of a hurricane.

But I could. I could do that. If not for me, for him. And for Lyric, who looked like he needed an escape from reality, no matter how brief.

"Okay."

Lyric's confident smile slipped just a fraction of an inch, like he hadn't really thought I'd say yes, but it was back in full force a millisecond later.

"Really? You'll get a drink with me?"

"Unless there's another definition of 'okay' that I'm not familiar with, then yes, that's what I meant."

Confusion. Excitement. Awe. All these emotions and more burned through his eyes, one after another, before he reached out to offer me his hand.

I didn't question it. I didn't even hesitate. I threaded my fingers through his and let him lead the way.

# Chapter Fifteen

## Lyric

We sat in the quiet diner for hours, just talking. Quinn wasn't much of a drinker, and neither was I, so instead of going to a bar, we settled for milkshakes in a mom and pop place in South Chicago.

It had been so long since I'd had a real, in-depth conversation with someone who didn't know my life, my background, my quirks- that I was finding it a little intimidating. Quinn was nothing like the women I'd spent time with over the years. She wasn't flaky or soft spoken. She was real. Confident. Interesting. Unshakable. She was amazing.

"So, what was she like, your sister?"

I spread my arms open wide and gestured up and down my body. "Pretty much the exact opposite of all this."

"Ah, she didn't have that smoldering hippie

vibe goin' on?" She asked, half joking.

"Not after she got out on her own, no. She was more, like... well, you. Drove my parents crazy. Drove me crazy at first, if I'm being completely honest, but I was just worried she was trying to be something she wasn't. It never occurred to me that she had spent her entire life being who she thought she had to be to fit in. When she moved here, she was finally able to be herself." I stopped, took a deep breath, and confessed something I wasn't particularly proud of. "Actually, the last time I saw her, I was pretty brutal. The-the last thing I said to her..." I broke off, shaking my head.

I couldn't believe that the last time my sister was alive and in my presence, I'd snubbed her. What kind of brother was I? I had just walked out the door. Well, technically, I'd slammed the door in her face.

I should have stayed. I should have talked things through with her and wrapped her in my arms and told her how much I loved her and how proud I was of her before I left. And now... I would never get a second chance to tell her how unbelievably exceptional she was.

A warm, comforting hand glided its way over mine and I looked up to see Quinn smiling sadly.

"Doesn't matter."

"What doesn't matter?" I asked, sniffing back tears.

"Whatever happened the last time you saw her, it doesn't matter. You seem like a loving guy, and I'm sure you did a million things over the course of her life to ensure that she knew just how much you cared about her. One rocky visit doesn't mean she thought you loved her any less. I mean, if I could write out all the times Ryan and I were at each others throats... the list would be endless. But it was only because we loved each other so fiercely that we fought. We always wanted what we thought was best for the other, and when one of us thought the other fell short, well... we fought. But that doesn't mean we loved each other any less. It means we loved each other more."

*Wow...*

The way the woman put all my doubts to rest with just a few sentences was amazing. Of course Mercy knew I loved her. She had to. No, we didn't have any 'Sibling of the Year' awards resting on our shelves, but we had always been there for each other. She always wanted the best for me, she was always looking out for me- even though I was the older brother. It had been *my* job to look after *her*. At least, that's what our parents had said to us growing up.

But Mercy possessed a nurturing, maternal instinct that marveled any kind of protectiveness I felt over her. She had always been the one looking out for me. Protecting me. Usually from myself.

Clearing my throat, I pulled my hand away back into safer territory. If we kept talking about Mercy, I wasn't sure I'd be able to hold it together.

"What do you do anyway? For work, I mean. Because you'd be one hell of a therapist."

"I'm a bank teller," she answered, as if it were the most awesome job on the planet.

"Woo, you must be a wild one. I can just imagine the crazy work parties you must throw." I waved my hands in the air, pretending to dance. "Watch out, Mrs. Callahan brought Zimas!"

I jumped as a shrill pain ran up my shin, and I realized I'd been hit.

"Did you just kick me?" I asked incredulously as I lowered my arms. "Seriously?"

"And if I did?" She shrugged her shoulders, challenging me, letting me know she wasn't one to back down.

"I guess I'd have to say now I know better than to mess with you. What are those, anyway? Steel-toed boots?" I reached down to rub the sting out of my leg.

"Could be," she said, laughing as she stirred the straw in her vanilla milkshake that had been close to empty for quite some time.

We both fell into a companionable silence as the smiles slowly left our lips. Yes, it was all fine and well when we were joking, but once the reality of our circumstances resurfaced, our grief threatened to unhinge us once again.

"It's hard, isn't it?" I looked up into Quinn's hazel eyes and instantly knew what she was referring to. There was no guess work involved. Every ounce of pain, every struggle, every tear she'd ever shed over her brother was right there beneath the surface, fighting to break free. "I barely remember going to Ryan's funeral. The service, the burial, person after person approaching me to tell me how sorry they were for my loss. It's all a blur."

"Because you were numb," I said. "Your body and mind just checked themselves into self-preservation mode so you could go on living, get through it without breaking."

"No." She shook her head as her eyes hardened in resigned conviction. "I still broke.

Something in me snapped after he died and I'm not sure if I'll ever feel," she paused, searching for the word, "whole. I doubt I'll ever feel like a whole person again."

"I can see that," I said, nodding, "but I don't agree. You seem pretty whole to me."

A sad smile pulled at the corner of her lips before they dropped again and began to tremble. It didn't matter what I said, there were a million variables I wasn't aware of that could make her cry at the drop of a hat. I knew that, because I was fighting the same battle.

"Hey." I reached for her hands. "No tears, alright? Everything happens for a reason. Ryan leaving was painful, but you have to look at the bigger picture."

"What bigger picture?" Quinn's voice trembled, and I wanted nothing more than to scoot the table out from between us and take her in my arms.

"The bigger picture. The grand scheme of things. Look, losing Mercy hurts like nothing I've ever felt before, but I have to believe she died for a reason. If I don't keep that in mind, I won't be able to deal with myself. I won't be able to cope. I have to think that she was part of something bigger, something important. There *has* to be a reason she was taken."

"And what if there's not?" She shot back, pulling her hands away. "What if the only reason they died was because life's not fair. They were taken," she snapped her fingers, "just like that. They are never coming back and there's a hole in my heart the size of Australia that I'll never be able to fill."

"That's okay." I grabbed for her hands again, and held tight when she tried to pull away. "There's nothing wrong with that. As long as your heart keeps beating, that's all that matters, enormous hole or not."

"You're an enormous hole," she grumbled back.

I knew I was getting to her. Even though we'd fallen back into serious talk, she still made a joke at my expense. That was a skill Mercy had mastered by the age of three.

Glancing up at the clock on the diner wall, I realized I had somewhere to be.

"Do you wanna head back to your car?"

Quinn let out a slow, even breath. "Yes. I think that's a good idea."

"Okay."

I threw a few bills on the table, enough to cover our shakes, and escorted her out the door with my hand at the small of her back. Once outside, I didn't want to let go, so I steered her all the way to my truck.

Once she was safely inside, I stood at the passenger door and watched her fasten her seat belt. I didn't understand the pull I felt towards her, but I also didn't question it. I didn't want to let her go.

"What are you doing tonight?"

"Tonight? Nothing, why?"

"Well, what about right now?"

"I'm sitting in your truck," she answered with a wry smile.

*Duh.*

"No, I mean, if you weren't with me. Would you have somewhere else to be? Am I- am I keeping

205

you from something important?" I'm not sure why I sounded so insecure all of a sudden, but I wanted to take Quinn with me on my next stop. But it wasn't a visit I took lightly. It would be hard as hell on me, but it would probably be equally hard on Quinn, revisiting memories I was sure she kept locked up tight somewhere in the many chambers of her heart.

"I would be at home, probably reading. Why?"

"I was wondering if you'd want to help me with something?" I ran a nervous hand through my hair, and she followed my movement, confused by my sudden change in demeanor.

"I... guess?"

I'd take that.

"Great." I shut her door and jogged around to my side. "But if at any point you want to go home, you just say the word and I'll drop what I'm doing and take you back to your car. Deal?" I held my hand out and she placed her small hand in mine without hesitation.

"Deal."

# Quinn

I trusted Lyric. I'm not sure why, but there was just something that soothed me about his presence- an instinctual feeling of safety I hadn't questioned. That is, until we pulled up next to the Chinatown Apartments.

Stepping out onto the curb, my heart began racing a marathon at the pace of about ten billion miles per hour. Tears sprang to my eyes as a barrage of questions burned through my mind at the sight of the place my twin brother took his last breath.

Why would he bring me here?

How did he know?

Why would he do that to me?

What was in it for him?

How could one person be so cruel?

Vision cloudy with disbelief, I turned to Lyric. "What are we doing here?" I managed to ask.

As if he weren't in the process of ripping my heart straight from my chest, he pocketed his keys and headed for the door. "I have to go up and get a few boxes. That okay?"

Lyric seemed totally oblivious to my plight, which told me that he had no idea how significant this building was to me. So, instead of screaming and running off down the street like I wanted to, I found myself nodding and following him inside, even though I could barely control my breathing. There were a lot of apartments here, surely I wouldn't even have to step foot on Ryan's floor. It would be okay. Everything would be okay... It had to be.

Going inside, we were greeted by a deserted lobby. Thanking my lucky stars I didn't have to converse with Mrs. Whitlock -because I surely would have broken down- I followed Lyric up the stairs and cringed as he pushed through the door on the third floor.

*It's fine. Everything is fine. No need to panic. You're doing fine, Quinn. Just follow him in, get whatever he needs, and then get the heck out. That's it. Keep it together. You'll be fine.*

Wrong.

Wrong. Wrong. Wrong.

"Is this some kind of joke?"

My voice was about a thousand decibels too high for the tiny hallway, but I'd had enough. I was a fool. Lyric had somehow led me into a trap. An emotional trap. But why? Why on earth would one person do that to another? And he had seemed so sweet. So normal. So... not evil.

"Excuse me?" The look on Lyric's face told me he was either stunned, hurt, or one hell of a good actor.

"This isn't funny, Lyric," I said, voice shaking.

"I don't know how you know, or why you would even do this to me, but this is the sickest-"

"Whoa!" He held his hands up to stop me. "What are you talking about? Knew what?"

"This is Ryan's apartment!" I finally cried, slamming my fist against the door.

Lyric, taking a step back, like he needed to distance himself from my level of crazy, shook his head in disbelief. "No, this is Mercy's apartment."

*What?*

*No.*

*That's... well, that's absurd.*

"I'm serious," I said, lowering my voice to a shaky whisper. "This isn't funny. Whatever you're trying to pull, stop it. Right now."

Lyric let out a breath before raking his hands through his hair in frustration, and that's when I noticed the key. He had a key, an actual key to the apartment door.

"I'm not trying to *pull* anything, Quinn," he said sadly. "Mrs. Whitlock asked me to come get the last few boxes of Mercy's things my parents weren't able to fit in their car."

Pocketing my rage for a moment to consider his words, I looked away from the door and braced myself to stare into Lyric's eyes, to get some kind of a reading on the situation. But what I expected to find, and what I was faced with, turned out to be two very different things.

Hurt. Betrayal. Grief. Loss. Anger. They fell, one after another, down Lyric's cheeks in the form of tears. He wasn't lying. This was really Mercy's apartment.

And Ryan's.

What were the odds?

One in infinity.

Together, we both turned to face the door, both filled to the brim with questions there would never be answers to. Both shaking, both scared, both completely lost- we stared at the tarnished gold thirty-three hanging on the door.

"Impossible," I heard Lyric say under his breath.

My thoughts exactly. Impossible.

I turned to face this still-stranger, knowing I owed him an apology.

"I'm so sorry, Lyric. I didn't mean to-"

Cutting me off mid-sentence, Lyric rushed forward to pull me into his arms, enveloping me in a crushing hug. Normally, I shied away from physical contact, especially with people outside of my family, but with Lyric, everything was different.

It felt... right. Like everything was going to be okay. His warmth seeped through every layer of clothing between us and instantly calmed my heart, calmed my hatred of the unfairness of the world.

"This means something," Lyric whispered into my hair. "It has to."

Maybe it did. Maybe it didn't. But I didn't have the mental or emotional capacity to question it. Maybe it was just a weird coincidence that both of our siblings had lived in the same apartment months before their deaths. Or maybe it wasn't coincidence. Maybe it was something else. Something stronger.

Either way, I didn't know how to make heads or tails of the situation. All I knew was that with

Lyric's arms wrapped around my shoulders, I felt stronger than I had in months.

And maybe *that* meant something.

Lyric hesitantly released me, and I could tell by the tremor of his shoulders he was through being strong, he was done putting on a front. So, taking the key from his hand, I unlocked the door and pushed it open. Offering him my hand, I smiled and nodded once in encouragement, letting him know that he was strong enough to do this. I hadn't been, but I was now. And maybe it wasn't Ryan's belongings we were packing up, but the symbolism and the feelings behind it were all the same.

"C'mon, you can do this," I urged. "We'll do it together."

So, hand in hand, soul in soul, we walked through the door.

Together.

# EPILOGUE
*Two Years Later*

# Lyric

Getting Quinn a diamond engagement ring seemed like a good idea at the time.

When the stone was cutting into my flesh as she held my hand while delivering our baby girl- it didn't seem like the brightest idea I'd ever had. But I ignored it. She was trying so hard, giving it her all. And I was in the sixth circle of hell watching her face contort in pain.

"Keep it up, baby. You're doing so good," I encouraged.

"Yes, Mrs. Callahan, you're doing great." The doctor's voice came from her perch between my soon-to-be wife's legs. "Just keep it up. Remember, you're doing this for your baby girl. For little..." The doc cut off, realizing we hadn't told her a name.

"We haven't decided yet," I explained.

One of the nurses holding Quinn's legs

212

chuckled, but I ignored her. Yes, I realized that going through nine months of pregnancy and sixteen hours of labor and still not agreeing on a name was ridiculous, but that's where we were.

"Are... are your parents here yet?" Quinn said through heavy panting.

"No, baby, but yours are. Do you want me to go get your mother?"

She tightened her grip on my hand, sending the diamond further into my flesh, and it took everything in my power not to cry out.

"No!" She ground out. "I don't need my mother. I need YOUR mother!"

My mother and Quinn had spent hours together practicing breathing exercises and pain management techniques, but I hadn't realized they'd grown *that* close.

"I'll go check and see if they're here yet."

"No!" She tightened her hold. Again. "No, you can't leave me."

"Okay, okay, I'm not going anywhere." I used my free hand to smooth the hair away from her damp forehead. "I'm not leaving," I whispered. "Ever."

"Never ever," she chanted back. On cue with the monitor above her bed, Quinn cried out in pain as another contraction tore through her body.

I'd never felt so helpless in all my life. Never. The woman I loved was in pain, and there wasn't a single thing I could do about it. No amount of hand-holding. No whispered words of encouragement. Nothing.

But the pain had a purpose... and that purpose was crowning.

"C'mon, Mrs. Callahan, you're doing great. Just keep it up, just like that, Quinn. Two more hard pushes and she'll be here. One!..."

Quinn clamped down around the breath she was holding and focused every drop of energy she still had on the job at hand. With a pale, blotchy face, ratted brown hair, bloodshot eyes- she looked like a woman who was enduring the worst form of torture ever invented. And yet, she was just as beautiful as the day we met. More so, actually.

Breath catching in her throat, she threw her head back on the pillow as the contraction subsided. Fat tears rolled down her cheeks and I kissed them away, one by one. She was wearing out fast, but we were so close to the finish line.

"C'mon, baby. One more push. Just one more. You've got this, okay? You've got it. Ready?" I looked to the doctor, who nodded, before locking eyes with Quinn.

"Ready." Her steely resolve flew through every limb as a determined light entered her eyes.

"Okay, here we go," the doctor instructed. "One BIG push. One! Two! Three..."

And that was it.

She was here.

As the doctor handed her off to a nurse, my eyes followed as they cleaned her under the blinding fluorescent light.

My heart swelled in my chest, threatening to cut off the breath I couldn't quite catch. My happiness fired out and came sweeping back after bouncing off the delivery room walls.

She was here.

Finally here.

And she was beautiful.

Just like her mother.

Holding Quinn's hand, kissing her forehead, her cheek, her lips as we watched our baby girl cry her first tiny, angelic note- something within me clicked into place.

For years, I'd wandered from place to place, state to state, never feeling wanted or needed. Never feeling like I belonged. But seeing those hazel eyes open for the first time... I felt it.

THIS was my calling. Being Quinn's future husband. Being this exquisite child's father. That was my lot in life. I'd spent my entire life searching for something without really knowing where to look... and now I'd found it.

# Quinn

Occasionally, Lyric had turned his back on me to take in a deep breath to center himself, but that was okay. It was to be expected. But he never left. He never let go. He was with me the whole time. And I'd been clinging to him like he was my only tie to earth- the only thing keeping me from floating away. Hell, maybe that's what he was.

Whatever had brought us together had been something strong, unstoppable. Something so much bigger than the two of us. And did we ever question it? No. Because we were just that happy. And thankful. So incredibly thankful.

It hadn't taken much for me to fall head over heels in love with the man, but he kept surprising me. Everyday was something more, something greater. With every hour I spent with Lyric, my love for him kept surprising me with it's expansion. And now, he'd given me the ultimate life.

A proposal- to which I'd hastily answered 'yes'.
A child- a beautiful, hazel eyed daughter.

I couldn't ask for more.

We had spent months fighting over a name. I had been insistent on her having the perfect name, but nothing came to mind, and everything anyone suggested I immediately shot down. Even Lyric had poured through every baby name book he could find and -being the control freak my maternal hormones had turned me into- I shot down name after name, even ones he had his heart set on.

But gazing down at the beautiful creature nestled in my arms... I knew it was time to give.

It was time for me to loosen the reins and let the man I trusted with my heart make a very important decision.

"Let's play a game," I quietly suggested as our baby girl slept in my arms.

"Okay," Lyric said, surprised and maybe a tad confused by my words.

"Grab the book."

I nodded toward my overnight bag. I didn't have to specify- he knew what book I was talking about.

As he settled back into the armchair beside the bed, I smiled conspiratorially as he held the book in his hands.

"You pick a name. Any name. Don't tell me what it is, just what it means."

Lyric lowered his brows, unsure of where I was headed. "How is this a game?"

"The meaning of the name can't be totally out there, okay? I don't want our daughter to be like, 'fruit bearer' or anything like that, but just pick a name that you love- one with a beautiful meaning."

"And?"

"And I'll say yay or nay to just the meaning and the first yay we come across will be it."

He cocked his head to the side. "You're serious?"

"As a heart attack."

"You really wanna play this game?"

"Yes," I answered with a nod. "BUT I have unlimited veto power."

Lyric rubbed a hand over his tired face and let out a slow laugh. "Of course you do. On anything and everything."

"Ha-ha, very funny. Now open the book."

My soon-to-be husband did as he was told and started flipping to pages he'd dog-eared.

"Of the resurrection, of springtime." He pushed his lips to the side and waited.

I didn't take long to respond. "Uh, no."

"Okay." He flipped a few more pages. "Bringer of joy."

"Nah."

Grumbling, he kept flipping. "Unexalted, impure." His lips twitched up at the corners.

"Are you trying to be funny?" I asked. "Because you suck at it."

He chuckled, shaking his head. "Sorry. Okay, how about... determined guardian?"

For a few moments, I let that meaning roll around my head. As much time as Lyric and I had spent talking about guardian angels, about how we could sometimes *feel* our loved ones around us, it just felt right. Something about it just clicked. It would be an homage to our lost siblings.

"Actually, yeah. I like that. A lot."

"You do?" He asked, surprised I wasn't still putting up a fight.

"Absolutely," I assured him as I took his hand in mine. "So, what is our daughter's name?"

Lyric leaned over and brushed a lock of brown hair off our slumbering child's face.

As he spoke her name for the first time, I looked down at sleeping eyes that, when opened, would favor her mother. Dark locks that had swirls of both light and dark brown. Fair skin that was the same shade as her father's. Lips that bowed just like her aunt Mercy's. And a brow that stayed furrowed as she slept- like she was working through all the ways of the world as she dreamed. That was all Ryan.

Losing Ryan was the single hardest thing I'd ever had to endure. Losing Mercy almost destroyed Lyric. But we had always had a deep, silent understanding that even though what happened to them was horrible, and in no way fair, it also brought about something that wouldn't have happened if it weren't for their deaths.

The little girl nestled against my chest would never have taken her first breath had I not met Lyric at the cemetery just minutes after Mercy's funeral. Yes, the circumstances were crushing and unconventional, but not every love story has a flawless beginning.

And flawed or not, our love brought about the fragile life in my arms.

"It's perfect," I breathed. "Willa Hunter."

Lyric pressed his forehead to mine and the three of us shared a beautiful, blissful, snapshot-worthy moment before he pulled away to speak our daughter's full name for the first time.

"Willa Myan Hunter."

The End

## Note from the Author

Saving Mercy wasn't a book I planned to write. The idea for Mercy and Ryan's love story formed one night as I was falling asleep and I jotted it down, but once I reread it in the morning, I decided to file it away in my 'not so great idea' pile. The only reason I revisited it was because someone convinced me to try writing a paranormal romance.

I knew I wasn't cut out for vampires, werewolves, witches, and wizards. So, where did that leave me? Ghosts...

Let me just say, I am SO INCREDIBLY GRATEFUL someone talked me into writing this book. It's my first venture into YA and, out of all the books I've written, Saving Mercy surpassed any and all of my expectations. It doesn't even resemble the notes I took down on that first night when the idea was born. It transcended into something entirely different.

This book means a lot to me, and I hope it will mean a lot to you as well.

If you liked the book (or even if you didn't) I would greatly appreciate a review. Reviews are SO IMPORTANT to indie authors.

Thanks for reading Saving Mercy, thanks for supporting me, and thanks for being awesome.

-N

# Acknowledgments

As always, I'd like to thank my family for supporting me through the book writing process. (I know you hate that I'm a hermit, sorry!) I know this book took longer to write than any other, but I really had to tip-toe around Mercy and Ryan's relationship. Hopefully, all that time shut up in my office alone will pay off. Love you guys!

There's also one other person who deserves a HUGE shout out. My buddy Ashley. I can, without a doubt, say that this book would NOT have happened without you. All those times when you gave me great ideas or got excited about a scene I was writing... that energy was what made me eager to write.

For all the times you let me bounce ideas off you, for the nights you stayed up late talking me through the emotional issues of these two people, for the random bursts of excitement over a line or appearance of a character, and for all those times you stared at paragraphs and attempted to help rearrange things I knew were wonky... thank you. Thank you so freaking much! Love you, Ash!

**Other Books by Nicole Tillman**

*One Vibrant Hue*

*Steady*

*The Blood Pawn*


PARANORMAL PEACEKEEPERS Series
*Whisper in the Rain*
*Scream in the Wind*
*Cry in the Fog*
*Sin in the Storm*
*Dance in the Hellfire*

## About the Author

Nicole Tillman is an author who hasn't always had a love of reading. As a child, she struggled to string words together and would hide in the back of the classroom with her head down in hopes that the teacher would forget she existed. Eventually, she was introduced to a young adult series by a family friend and her love of reading bloomed.

Nicole now weaves her own stories, content to lose sleep in order to write both contemporary romance and thriller/suspense novels. She lives in the Ozarks of Missouri with her husband, two sons, and two dogs.

Nicole has an Associates Degree in General Studies though Missouri State University and was on her way to completing her Bachelors in Creative Writing when she decided to take a sabbatical to focus on work and her family. Now a stay at home mother, she dedicates her time to her boys, writing, and photography.

Made in the USA
Monee, IL
21 April 2024

57284989R00128